JINGLED—A SCI-FI ALIEN WARRIOR ROMANCE HOLIDAY NOVELLA

TRIBUTE BRIDES OF THE DREXIAN WARRIORS #7

TANA STONE

BROADMOOR BOOKS

CHAPTER
ONE

Reina bustled down the corridor, her shoes echoing off the shiny floor as she took long steps. She touched a spindly hand to the bobbing blue swish of hair that extended over her head and sighed.

The human women were at it again.

As a tribute bride liaison, she was used to handling requests from the human females the Drexians brought up to the space station. It wasn't unusual for her to deal with everything from hysteria to disbelief to anger when the Earthlings learned they'd been abducted from their planet to be brides for a warrior race of aliens. Although most of the women were eventually happy with the arrangement—especially after they saw the hunky Drexians—Reina was not unaccustomed to drama.

As a Vexling—a species known for their attention to detail and desire to please—her instinct was to solve every problem and keep everyone happy. And she really did want her tribute brides to be happy, although sometimes she wished they didn't rope her into *every* scheme they came up with. She'd been involved in last-minute bridal showers, surprise weddings, and even a gender-reveal party one tribute had insisted on. Humans' need to know the gender of

1

their children so they could then dress them in certain colors baffled her, but she'd gone along with it.

And now this.

She reached the inclinator and swiped her hand over a panel to one side, waiting for a moment before the compartment doors swished open, and she stepped inside between a Gatzoid tapping away on a tablet and a Neebix holding his tail politely in front of him.

The inclinator was crowded today, no doubt everyone busy as the space station got back to normal operations. It had been many weeks since the station—known by most as the Boat—had taken on new tribute brides, or even allowed incoming transports of Drexians. The attacks by their enemy, the Kronock, along with sabotage of the station and the discovery of traitors within the Drexian leadership, had kept them on high alert. Like everyone, she was glad things were returning to normal, although the latest request by the tribute brides was *not* normal.

"Reina?"

She turned and spotted another Vexling at the back of the compartment, his nearly transparent hair extending high above the other heads. Her pulse fluttered, and she hoped her gray cheeks did not betray her surprise and pleasure at seeing Vivan.

"Greetings of the day to you," she said, extending the formal Vexling greeting, since they were in the company of so many others.

"Thank you," he said, as he wiggled his way to stand next to her at the front of the compartment that surged upward. "To you, as well."

Reina darted a quick glance at the fellow Vexling. Like all of her species, he was tall and lanky, although Reina had always thought that Vivan had a squarer jaw than most Vexling males. She knew he worked in the station's procurement department, determining what items were needed from Earth during the transports to the surface to obtain tribute brides. Vivan had often been the one to

2

help her, when her brides required something specific and did not want a holographic version.

The Boat relied on sophisticated holographic technology to create much of the fantasy settings for the humans, but some things could not be manufactured by light diffraction. That was why the space station had an entire department devoted to procuring specific items from Earth to make the human women feel at home. Since they were the key to the Drexian's survival, their happiness was paramount.

"You must be busy," Reina said.

Vivan nodded. "It has been many cycles since a transport returned from Earth. We are eager for its arrival." He focused his gaze on her. "You must also be glad to receive new tribute brides."

"Of course," Reina said, although truthfully, she was relieved the brides would not be arriving that day.

Despite loving her job, she had welcomed the slower pace of things when the transports of the tribute brides had been halted. Her work partner, Serge, had grown increasingly impatient not having a wedding to plan. She, however, had enjoyed getting to know some of her recent brides, instead of having to immediately move on to the next arrival.

Vivan's large eyes studied her. "You seem worried, Reina."

"Not worried." She shook her head. "Perplexed. Maybe you can help me."

He took her hand. "You know I will always help you."

Reina knew her cheeks were flushing as the inclinator door opened, and she was grateful when everyone around them exited. She and Vivan did not step off, and the doors slid shut again, although the compartment did not move.

"Reina?" His voice was quiet, but it made her jerk her head to meet his gaze.

All Vexling eyes were gold, yet his seemed more luminous to her. She swallowed and tried to focus her mind. What did she need to ask him? It had seemed important, but now she couldn't remember.

Think, Reina. She closed her own eyes to shut out the distraction of Vivan's.

"Christmas," she said, her eyes snapping open.

"Christmas?" he repeated, tilting his head at her.

"A human holiday," she went on. "We've had tributes want to celebrate it before, but usually they did it in their suites. Now a group of my brides want to throw a station-wide Christmas party."

"That sounds intriguing." He did not drop her hand. "What is involved in a Christmas party?"

"From what I can gather there is a lot of food, many drinks, singing songs called carols, and presents given out by a fat, human man wearing red."

Vivan's high forehead wrinkled. "We do not have any fat male humans, nor do I think it would be practical to procure any."

"From what I understand, humans often dress like this fat man, and use padding to look larger than they are."

Vivan's blinked a few times. "Fascinating. As long as I have been procuring things from Earth, I continue to be surprised by what humans enjoy. One day I will have to tell you about the Slinky."

"I would like that," Reina said, jumping slightly as the inclinator doors opened, and a pair of Drexian warriors entered.

Vivan dropped her hand, and they moved to the back of the compartment as the Drexians activated the inclinator and it rotated before accelerating.

"How can I help with this Christmas party?" Vivan asked in a low voice, as the Drexians discussed the Kronock.

"I don't suppose we have any tall, pointy trees on the station?" Reina asked, looking ahead.

"Do trees have something to do with the fat human in red?"

Reina tried to recall what Mandy and Bridget had said about the trees. Christmas trees, they'd called them. They'd both been talking so fast that it had been hard to make sense of it all. "I think they cover the trees with balls and the fat man puts the presents around the bottom."

"This is very strange indeed," Vivan muttered. "I can see why you are concerned."

"The tribute brides want to have this Christmas party on the promenade in a week's time. I'd hate to tell them no, especially since some of them have been through quite a lot."

"I heard about the reject who was rescued from the Kronock hybrid. I am glad she is all right." Vivan glanced at her. "After all the things that have happened on the station, maybe a party would be good for everyone."

The inclinator stopped and the two Drexians got off. Vivan also stepped off. "I should get to work before they send out someone to procure *me*."

Reina giggled. "Of course."

"I will see what I can do about these Christmas things," he said, giving her a small bow with his head before starting to walk away.

Reina shot a hand between the inclinator doors before they closed. "Would you come?"

Vivan turned back around. "Come?"

"To the party?" Reina asked before she could think better of it.

A small smile curled his gray lips. "If you will be there, I would not miss it."

Reina let the doors close and sagged against the walls of the compartment, her hands fluttering at her throat. Now she had more than the Christmas party to worry about.

CHAPTER
TWO

D orn clung to the ladder that dangled into the holographic ocean outside his fantasy suite. The water was a blue so clear he could see all the way to the white-sand bottom, and his heart rate increased as he remembered sinking to the depths of the simulated South Pacific sea. "It sounds to me like you should be working on this party you and Bridget came up with, instead of torturing your mate."

"This is not torture. It's swimming."

Dorn grunted, clearly disagreeing with her assessment. "Explain to me again why I have to do this."

"Because you promised you'd let me teach you how to swim," his wife said from a few feet away where she treaded water in a shiny, gold bikini. "And because you almost drowned once already."

He shot her a look. "And why was that?"

She splashed him. "You deserved to get pushed in. You were being a dick."

He emitted a low growl, licking the salty beads of water from his lips. "And you were being stubborn and impossible."

"Yet look how far we've come." She gave him a wicked grin as she spread her arms wide and floated on her back, the slight swell of her pregnant belly poking above the water. "Who would have guessed that we could have gone from almost killing each other to being deliriously happy and expecting our first baby?"

Dorn felt a rush of emotion as he watched his mate and the child she carried in her belly. After years of commanding the Inferno Force on the outskirts, he'd never imagined that he would have anything close to the happiness he'd found with his human. Before he'd been assigned a tribute bride, he'd been happy leading his rough group of warriors and content finding scraps of pleasure in victory. Now, everything was different. He was different. He cleared his throat. "Not me."

"Dorn," Mandy said, her voice becoming stern as she swam closer. "You've practiced in the plunge pool. You know the strokes. You can do this. Besides, I need to meet Bridget soon to work on the party, so let's move it, big guy."

He scowled at her, and then looked longingly at the fluffy towels stretched out across the pair of loungers on the teakwood deck, wishing he were there, instead of in the water. "Drexians do not have..." he paused, searching for the unfamiliar word, "Christmas."

"Not until now, you mean," Mandy corrected. "I promise that you'll love it. Presents, songs, cookies. It's the best. And if anyplace needs a little Christmas spirit, it's the Boat."

She might have a point there, Dorn thought. Morale on the station had been low since the Kronock attack and the discovery of a mole inside the Drexian leadership. A party might help, even if it was for a strange human holiday. He sighed as he eyed the water around him. "You promise not to be excessive with this party."

"Excessive?" She gave him an expression of mock horror. "When have you ever known me to be excessive?"

He cocked an eyebrow at her, and she laughed.

"Fine, I'll keep it under control. I may not have a choice. It's not like this place is brimming with holiday decor. We're probably going to have to have Ella do everything holographically."

"How is the reject adjusting to not being a reject anymore?"

Dorn asked, eyeing the crystal-clear water suspiciously. He knew his friend Dakar was thrilled to be living with the human who'd once rejected being a tribute bride, but he hadn't seen much of the human herself, since they'd returned from their rescue mission to save another reject bride from a rogue cyborg Drexian.

"She's great. I may even convince her to have a Christmas wedding." Mandy dipped her hair back in the water. "But enough stalling. It's time for you to show me what you've got, big guy."

"Come closer, and I will show you what I've *got,* mate."

Wagging a finger at him, she stayed out of his reach. "Nice try. You want to get some before I have to go meet Bridget? You'd better start swimming."

Mandy would make an effective commander, he thought, with a mixture of annoyance and admiration. She was certainly more confident than she'd been when she'd first arrived on the station. Back then, she'd been insecure and frightened, and she'd tried to hide it by being demanding and difficult. It was almost hard to remember how different she'd been before she'd finally opened up to him, made friends with the other tribute brides, and found her place on the Boat

He glanced back at her. "If I sink to the bottom again, you will not be able to retrieve me in your condition."

"First of all," she said. "I'm pregnant, not infirm. And if you're really worried, I guess you'll just have to be sure you don't sink."

"You're still impossible," he said, the corners of his mouth quirking, despite his best intentions.

"So you've told me." She clapped her hands, sending a small spray of water into the air. "More swimming. Less talking."

Dorn knew the only way to shut her up was to actually swim. He took a deep breath and pushed off from the ladder, pulling his arms through the water as his body dipped below the surface. Kicking his legs forcefully, he was propelled to Mandy within seconds.

"You did it!"

She looked so happy, Dorn couldn't help but feel proud of

himself. He slowed and started to scissor his feet under him like her, and soon he was bobbing upright in the water.

"I knew you could do it." Mandy threw her arms around him and for a moment, his body sank under the surface. He kicked harder and resurfaced, wrapping an arm around his mate and keeping both of their heads out of the water.

She laughed and swiped her face, flicking drops off. "Sorry. I got too excited."

"I like it when you are excited."

Her expression shifted from excited to wary to amused. "Oh, no." She fluttered her feet as she attempted to kick away from him. "I know what that look means."

Dorn moved one hand to touch the firm curve of her belly. "Don't worry. I cannot get you more pregnant than you already are. I am not a Krenginian."

"Good to know." She shook her head. "But I still have to meet Bridget in half an hour."

He swam them over to the ladder, spinning so that he sat on a rung submerged in water and pulling her to straddle him. "I am a Drexian warrior. I excel at efficiency."

She swatted him, wiggling, even though he held her in place by the hips. "You excel at distracting me and making me forget everything else."

He shrugged and assumed his most innocent expression, positioning her so that she rubbed against his hard cock. "Is it my fault that being with child has made you insatiable?"

Dropping her head back, she groaned. "I don't know what's wrong with me."

He let his gaze drift from her long brown hair streaming wet down her back, to her rounded breasts barely covered by the triangles of gold fabric. "Nothing is wrong with you. You are perfect."

Another groan, as she rocked forward, grinding against him through the fabric of their bathing suits. Dorn moved one hand from her belly to her face, cupping her jaw and dragging a finger across her lips.

She captured his finger in her mouth, sucking it as she looked down at him, her eyes burning with intensity.

Gods, he thought, as he watched her take his finger into her mouth. He fought to keep his own eyes from rolling up into the back of his head. Dipping his hand under the water, he pushed aside her bikini bottom and parted her soft folds, finding her wet nub and circling it with his thumb.

Mandy sucked harder on his finger, moving her hips and moaning.

Dorn swirled his thumb faster, and her movements became jerky. She leaned back, and Dorn pulled his finger from her mouth and moved it to one breast, slipping it under the bikini top and flicking her hard nipple. He sank a finger into her tight heat, while his thumb continued to circle her slick nub.

Mandy crushed her mouth to his, her kiss desperate as she writhed in his lap, her legs straddling his waist. He matched the strokes of his tongue to the strokes of his finger inside her, savoring the heat of both. Dorn increased his pace as he felt her body quiver and her hands claw at his shoulders.

Tearing away from the kiss, she threw her head back and bucked against him, her body spasming as it contracted around his finger. He felt the ripples as she came, watching her face contort in ecstasy and finally relax as she slumped onto him.

"Dorn." Her voice was soft and breathy.

"Yes, mate?" He lifted her by the hips again, this time holding her as he flipped her around so that she was on the stairs. Her elbows rested on the deck and her knees rested on one of the lower rungs. He tucked himself between her legs and untied one side of her bikini bottom.

"What are you doing?" she asked, twisting her head to watch the strings of her bikini fall apart.

He untied the other side and the gold fabric fell into the water. "I want to watch you take me."

She made a soft moan and arched her ass into the air, the water lapping around her thighs. "I'm so ready for you."

Dorn tugged his tight black suit down, letting his cock spring free. He dragged it through her hot, wet folds; pushing her head down with one hand and nudging her legs open wider. Seeing her spread for him was almost more than he could take, but he buried his cock inside her slowly, watching her stretch to take his girth as he pushed deep, savoring the feel of her tight heat and her desperate, keening sounds. Hands clasped on her hips, he thrust into her again, this time urgently.

"You like watching, don't you, Dorn?" she asked, her voice teasing. "You like seeing your big cock split me."

He could barely grunt out an answer as she rocked back into him, meeting him thrust for thrust. "You're so tight for me."

Mandy craned her neck so that her gaze met his. "Harder, Dorn."

Her command sent fire pounding through his veins, and he lost all ability for rational thought, pistoning into her as she cried out. He felt her as she splintered apart, her body tensing and convulsing moments before his own release blinded him. With a primal scream, he emptied into her. Breathing as if he'd run a race, Dorn braced himself against the deck so he wouldn't collapse on top of her.

The water slapped at the backs of his shaking legs as he wrapped one arm gently around her belly. "You sure it wasn't too hard?"

Mandy's face was flushed pink as she turned and gave him a drowsy smile. "I'm sure." She scooped up the bikini bottom floating near one of the steps and shifted so she was facing up. She gave him a long, soft kiss. "Now I really do need to run. This Christmas party isn't going to plan itself."

Dorn watched her walk bare-assed into their fantasy suite,

admiring the view. He pulled his own suit back up and flopped back into the water, letting himself float faceup as he caught his breath.

A lot had happened since he'd first arrived on the Boat, reluctant and angry and not at all eager to take a mate. He grinned as he listened to Mandy sing in the distance. He wouldn't change a thing.

CHAPTER

THREE

B ridget stretched and rolled over on the faux-fur rug in front of the crackling fire. The warmth on her face made her smile as she blinked a few times and tugged the soft blanket over one bare shoulder.

"You aren't trying to get up, are you?" Her mate, Kax, looped an arm around her waist and tugged her close to him. His voice sounded sleepy as he nuzzled his face in her neck, kissing her drowsily.

"I can't believe we fell asleep in front of the fireplace again."

"Good thing it's only a holographic fire." Kax continued planting featherlight kisses along her throat, causing Bridget to shiver with pleasure.

She glanced up at the wooden beams of the peaked ceiling and over to one of the large windows looking out onto a perfect ski slope. Snow fell softly outside—as it always did—but they were toasty-warm inside, the scent of the burning logs making it hard to believe the entire thing was a holographic projection.

For someone who'd lived in Florida for years and sweated her way through brutal summers, the alpine ski chalet was a heavenly escape, and one she'd only dreamt about before she'd been abducted by the Drexians and brought to their high-tech, holo-graphically tricked-out space station.

She'd never have imagined her life would have taken such a turn. From washed-out ballet dancer to tribute bride for an alien warrior. She wiggled closer to Kax. A really hot alien warrior.

"We should probably start using the bed," she said, laughing as she glanced over at the mahogany sleigh bed covered with luxurious linens.

"Probably," Kax murmured in her ear, nipping at the lobe and sending a jolt of pleasure through her. "But aren't bear skin rugs in front of fireplaces meant for lying on? Don't you humans have many movies where couples sleep on fur?"

"Yes," Bridget admitted, "but not many people sleep on them all the time."

"I see." Kax did not sound concerned. "We can certainly move to the bed, although I enjoy sitting with you in front of the fire."

Bridget loved it, too. They'd developed a routine since getting married. They would sit together in front of the fireplace at the end of the day and talk while they ate dinner and had a few glasses of Palaxian wine. The talk and the wine usually led to more, and they almost always ended up naked and rolling around on the fluffy white rug. To be honest, the rug was so soft and plush she didn't miss the bed, and you couldn't beat waking up in front of a crackling fire.

Since Kax occasionally left the station for classified missions with military intelligence, Bridget cherished mornings when they woke up together. There was nothing she loved more than the feel of his big arms around her, and the muscular curves of his chest pressing against her back.

"I can't sleep in today," she said, hating to break the spell as his lips tickled her ears. "I promised I'd meet Mandy to work on the Christmas party."

Kax brushed her dark hair off her shoulder before kissing it, too. "Right. Christmas. I take it this is an important holiday on Earth."

Bridget laughed. "Yeah, it's pretty big. Not everyone celebrates it religiously, but it's also a time for exchanging presents and doing nice things for other people. It used to be my favorite holiday. There's nothing quite like the excitement of Santa leaving presents for you when you're young."

Kax paused. "Used to be?"

She should have known he'd pick up on that. Kax was nothing if not attentive. Bridget pulled the blanket higher, as she felt a chill that had nothing to do with the perfectly moderated temperature in the chalet. "Christmas in the foster system wasn't always so great."

She'd told Kax about her childhood after her parents and then her grandmother had died, but she didn't like to talk too much about her saddest memories. She felt lucky to have been found by someone who adored her as much as Kax did, and it helped push those memories to the back of her mind, where they belonged.

"I am sorry." He buried his face in her neck from behind, squeezing her tight. "We will have to make sure this is the best Christmas you've ever had."

She nodded, not able to speak because of the lump that had formed in her throat. Of course, Kax would want to do everything he could to make her happy, even if he had no idea about Christmas or why it was so important to her and the other humans on the station.

"What would you think about playing Santa?" she asked, when she'd cleared her throat.

"Santa?"

Bridget rolled onto her back so she could look up at him. "He's the guy who gives out all the presents."

Kax grinned, the corners of his intense, green eyes crinkling. "I think I would like that."

She rubbed a hand across the stubble covering his cheeks. "You'd probably look pretty sexy in a white beard and red hat."

His eyebrows went up. "White beard? Is this Santa like a Merutog?"

Bridget cocked her head at him. "A Merutog?"

"A species noted for their long, white facial hair."

"The entire species? Even the females?"

Kax nodded. "The Merutog have three genders, but, yes, all of them have white beards."

Bridget laughed. She was still getting used to the concept of aliens, not to mention so many alien species she never could have imagined. "Santa isn't a Merutog, but he is old. He lives at the North Pole, which is cold and probably looks a lot like it does outside here. He flies around on a sleigh pulled by reindeer, and can deliver presents to millions of children in one night."

"So he's magic." Kax kissed her lightly on the nose. "I like the sound of this Santa."

"Then that's settled. You'll be Santa at the Christmas party. Now I just have to get the wedding-dress designers to whip up a Santa suit for you."

"Randi and Monti?" Kax asked, obviously remembering the colorful duo of dress designers.

"I know this isn't a glamorous wedding gown, but I think they may enjoy the challenge," Bridget said. "At least, I hope they will."

"You're a tribute bride," Kax reminded her. "You might be already mated to me, but everyone on the Boat still wants to make you happy. Not as much as I do, of course."

Bridget giggled as he shifted himself so he was on top of her. "You know Mandy's going to be here any second, right?"

"Dorn told me she was giving him another swimming lesson this morning," Kax said. "Knowing how difficult my brother is, she may have her hands full. I would not count on her being on time."

He lowered his mouth to hers, kissing her softly, his tongue teasing the tip of hers. Desire buzzed through her body, and she felt her own body's traitorous response, as her skin warmed and her nipples hardened. Despite her best intentions, she arched into him.

"I can never get enough of you." He pulled away, and his eyes were molten as he gazed down at her.

"I hope not, because you're stuck with me for life, tough guy." Bridget ran one hand through his short, honey-brown hair, pulling his face to hers again.

He moaned as he lowered his mouth to hers. Her other hand found the nodes along his spine, caressing them as his noises of arousal grew louder. She loved feeling the bumps harden and heat under her touch, and his groans made her stroke them even faster.

A loud beeping from the door jerked her from the haze of desire. Kax lifted himself off of her, his breath jagged. Bridget wiggled out from under him and hopped up.

"You have to go?" Kax stared at her as he flopped onto his back, his enormous cock tenting the blanket. "Now?"

Bridget eyed his massive erection and fought the urge to tell Mandy to take a hike. "Absence makes the heart grow fonder."

Kax sighed as he watched her walk naked toward the bathroom for a robe. "It would be impossible for me to be any fonder of you."

Bridget's cheeks warmed, and it had nothing to do with desire. She grabbed two robes off hooks inside the bathroom, tossing one to her mate. "I feel the exact same way, my sexy Santa."

CHAPTER
FOUR

K atie rolled over and felt the other side of the bed where Zayn's warm body should have been. Nothing. Pushing herself up and swiping her mass of strawberry-blonde curls out of her face, she peered out to the balcony and saw his massive silhouette leaning against the teakwood railing. He wore nothing but soft, drawstring pants that hung low on his waist, and her eyes were drawn to the nodes running down his spine—bumps that heated and hardened when he was aroused. Seeing him like this, taking in the morning view from their suite, made her wish she were an early riser.

She yawned and stretched, trying not to make noise. She didn't want to ruin the magical moment, although she knew it was all holographically created. The sunrise was still breathtaking—slats of sun peeking from over flat-topped trees in the horizon, sending golden rays across the tall grasses of the savannah; a cluster of antelope lazily walking by and birds flitting through the sky, one occasionally cawing in the distance; the scent of impending rain that rarely came. Katie knew all the holographic fantasy suites created for the tribute brides and their mates were beautiful, but she felt none could be as jaw-dropping as this.

As if he sensed her swinging her legs over the side of the bed, Zayn turned around. "You're up."

"Don't let me spoil the sunrise," she said, padding across the polished-teak floors to join him on the veranda that stretched around two sides of their high-tented suite.

Her mate grinned as he pulled her close to him, wrapping his big arms around her waist. "You could never ruin anything. You only make things better."

Katie's cheeks warmed, even though she should be used to his compliments by now. They'd been married for a couple of months already, and were still fully ensconced in the honeymoon phase, not that that was difficult, since they lived in a setting so luxurious and romantic most couples could only dream of visiting for a honeymoon. She pressed her cheek against his bare chest muscle, and traced a finger down one arm, bumping over the scars that crossed his forearms—a reminder of his time being held captive by the Kronock.

"You still can't sleep well?" she asked without looking up.

Since she'd known him, Zayn had suffered from nightmares and flashbacks having to do with the mission that had gone sideways and ended with his entire platoon being slaughtered by the Kronock and him being taken captive. Even though he didn't talk about it often, she knew the guilt still gnawed at him.

"I just enjoy mornings out here." He kissed the top of her head. "And I enjoy watching you sleep and listening to the little noises you make."

She swatted his chest. "I do not make noises when I sleep."

He laughed. "You do, and they're so soft and sweet it takes all my self-control not to crawl on top of you and give you a reason to make more noise."

Katie let her hand drift down to the taut ridges of his stomach. "You should wake me up."

He leaned back and looked down at her, his cerulean-blue eyes intense as he tangled a hand in her curls and pulled her into a deep kiss. Letting herself sink into it, she lifted her hands to loop around his neck. The warmth of his lips sent pleasure coursing through her body and had her arching into him, eager to feel his rigid length as it pressed against her hip.

"Well, we're both up now," she said when they separated, her voice nearly a purr.

He emitted a noise in the back of his throat that was part groan and part growl. "And I have to leave."

Katie jerked back. "Leave? Now? It's the crack of dawn."

Zayn grinned. "Actually, it's later than you think. I adjusted our holographic settings for later sunrises, since you enjoy sleeping late, but I am due on the bridge very shortly."

She was about to scold him for tricking her with the settings— although she appreciated the extra sleep—but then she felt a pang of guilt that she'd forgotten about today. His first day back as a fully commissioned Drexian warrior, and his first day working on the space station's command deck.

She knew how important it was to him to work again. After escaping from the Kronock, his adjustment back into Drexian life hadn't been smooth, and at one point he'd even been suspected of sabotage. Even though his name was cleared and he'd finally been given the go-ahead by the medical team to return to duty, it had taken a while for the Drexian leadership to decide where to put him. This appointment to the bridge was a big deal, and one that he fully deserved.

"That's right. I'm so sorry I forgot." She glanced back into the room. "Should I call for breakfast?"

He shook his head. "I'll grab something on the promenade. One of those stimulants you love so much."

Katie let out a breath. "Okay, as long as you understand that it's not *real* coffee."

"Understood." Zayn laughed, as he stepped out of his pants and walked toward the bathroom, leaving Katie to ogle his naked ass.

That view never gets old, she thought, as she watched him

disappear into the bathroom and heard the shower turn on. He was so hot and built and just all-around gorgeous that she still felt like shaking herself sometimes. Zayn was a far cry from her loser boyfriends on Earth. Actually, everything on the Boat was a far cry from her life back in L.A.

There, she'd been broke with pathetic job prospects, and law enforcement convinced she'd had something to do with the socialite Mandy Talbot's disappearance. Turns out, Mandy hadn't disappeared. She'd been abducted by aliens. She almost laughed as she thought about the gossip rags she'd worked for as a paparazzo. She didn't regret abandoning her plan to reveal the existence of the Drexian's space station, and their decades-long program of taking women from Earth, but she would love to see the looks on the slimeball editors' faces if they knew the truth. Especially that lowlife from the *Enquirer*.

She'd given that up, along with any hope of returning to Earth, when she'd decided to marry Zayn. A decision she'd never regretted for a moment.

"You okay?" Zayn asked, walking out of the bathroom with a beige towel wrapped around his waist, and droplets of water dripping off his short, dark hair.

Katie looked up, his voice snapping her out of her thoughts.

"What is that expression Serge used the other day?" Zayn pulled off his towel and rubbed it over his wet hair, crossing to the tall, wooden dresser and opening drawers. "A penny for your thinking?"

"Penny for your thoughts," Katie corrected him. "Serge may be an expert on weddings, but he's not the last word on Earth expressions."

Even though she'd seen her husband naked plenty, the sight of him never failed to impress her. He pulled on tight, black boxer-briefs, and her mouth went dry when she saw how well he filled them out. She flopped back on the bed, draping her arms over her head and letting her short, silk nightie ride up. "You sure you have to leave?"

Glancing back over his shoulder, Zayn bit his bottom lip. He pulled on dark uniform pants and a tight T-shirt, then took a couple of long strides to the bed, bracing his arms on either side of her and leaning down. He nipped her neck. "Positive, but I'll be back tonight."

Katie sighed, his warm breath sending shivers down her spine. "I'm counting on it."

He kissed her neck, inhaling deeply before standing back up. "Don't you have something to do with the other tributes today, anyway?"

Rolling over, Katie let out a huff of breath. "That. Yeah, I guess I do."

He chuckled as he returned to the dresser and pulled out a starched uniform jacket. "You don't sound excited. Mandy made me think this was something fun."

Katie knew that Zayn saw Mandy, one of the other tribute brides—and the woman she'd been suspected of kidnapping on Earth—when he went to the medical bay for periodic follow-ups from his surgery. Her fellow tribute bride worked there, and was training to be a medic. Even though Mandy was the reason she'd been abducted from Earth, Katie had made peace with the woman, and the two had even become good friends. That didn't mean she was on board for Mandy's latest idea.

She shrugged as she watched her mate fasten the sash filled with medals and commendations over his chest. "I guess Christmas isn't my thing."

"From what Mandy said, it is a very important holiday on your planet. One that most people love."

"Most people," Katie said. "Christmas was just never very merry when I was growing up."

She didn't tell him that the holidays had been a perfect occasion for her professional scam-artist father to go into high gear, roping her into schemes to bilk people out of bonuses and convince them to donate to fake charities. He'd considered the uptick in generosity to be the perfect time to run cons, while the whole thing had made her feel dirty. It had been bad enough that she'd never had a normal childhood and had learned to play Three-card Monte when most kids were playing Uno, but fleecing people at Christmas had made her feel even worse. She'd quickly learned to dread the season, and the knowledge that she and her father and his shady friends would be the cause of more than one miserable Christmas.

Zayn came up behind her and wrapped his arms around her waist, then bent down so that he could kiss her neck. "Then we will make sure this year will be different."

She wanted to believe him, but the knot in the pit of her stomach told her not to get her hopes up. What did an alien who'd never even celebrated Christmas know about the holiday? It had never brought anything but sadness for her, and she preferred to ignore it altogether. Somehow, she suspected with Mandy at the helm of the Boat's celebration, ignoring it would be hard to do this year.

Katie let out a sigh—half resigned, half hopeful. "Okay."

He kissed her again, before walking to the door and swiping his hand over the side panel to open it. "Have fun planning with the other brides."

"Good luck at work." She gave him her best smile, as he disappeared down the walkway with a final wave over his shoulder.

"Fun" and "planning" were not two words that went together for Katie, especially not having to do with Christmas. She resisted muttering "Bah Humbug" under her breath, as she headed for the bathroom and her own shower.

CHAPTER
FIVE

Even with her head practically inside the metal hull of the space ship, Trista heard the thudding boots as they crossed the floor of the flight deck. She didn't look up, though. Not when she was so close to figuring out why the thruster on this particular fighter continued to jam.

Drexian tech may have been significantly more advanced than that on Earth, but when it came down to it, machines were machines. She'd worked on enough bikes, trucks, and muscle cars to understand what made engines run. One advantage to dating guys who were in rough bike clubs on Earth. And if she was being honest, the only advantage.

Trista drummed her oil-stained fingers on the steel of the damaged engine. "What's got you all clogged up, baby?" she muttered.

"I wouldn't say clogged up." The deep voice said from right beside her. "More like dismayed to find my mate missing from my bed."

Trista jumped at the sound and banged her head on the metal engine hatch. She straightened and tipped her head back to look up at her husband's scowling face. "Don't sneak up on me like that, Torven."

He looked slightly wounded at her response. "I did not sneak up on you."

Okay, he was right about that. She'd heard his footsteps, she just hadn't known they were his, and hadn't cared. She'd been too absorbed in her work, a recurring theme since she'd been given access to the flight deck and permission to assist with repairs.

She was actually happy to see him, she thought, as she studied his severe expression with narrowed gold eyes. Despite his appearance—the shaggy dark hair, the thick tattoos swirling down one arm, the craktow tooth dangling from a leather cord around his neck, the massive muscles everywhere—she knew her husband wasn't as scary as he looked.

"Sorry." Trista popped up on her tiptoes to give him a quick kiss, as she tucked a strand of blonde hair back into her ponytail. "I'm just stuck with this thruster issue."

He eyed the black hull of the fighter. "So stuck you had to crawl out of bed in the middle of the night to come work on it?"

"It wasn't the middle of the night. It was almost light outside, and yes, I had to come try something."

Her kiss seemed to mollify him, and he uncrossed his arms. "Did it work?"

She let out a long breath. "No, but I'm not giving up."

"I would expect nothing less from my little grease monkey." Torven hooked an arm around her waist, and yanked her close so she was flush with him.

His nickname for her always made her smile. "Oh, yeah?"

She put her grease-stained hands on his chest, all hard curves and ridged muscle, and her pulse quickened. As much as she loved working on engines, she couldn't deny that the slightest touch by him could rev her up in a matter of seconds. She'd always had a thing for bad boys, although this bad boy was actually an honorable

Drexian warrior who would give his life for hers without thinking twice. Trista liked to think that falling for him had finally broken her streak of getting involved with the wrong kind of men who never treated her right. Torven treated her like a goddess. Well, a grease-monkey goddess.

"I'm proud of you." Torven ran a thick finger down her throat, stopping at the top closure of the Drexian version of coveralls she'd thrown on over her clothes. "You've shown everyone just how smart and hardworking you are. And how you don't take no for an answer."

"Thanks. I learned it from you."

He gave a low laugh as he unfastened the top of her coveralls to reveal a silky top. "You were headstrong and tough before I came along."

She shrugged, trying to ignore her rapid breathing as his finger wandered down and caressed the soft swell of one breast. "Maybe down deep, but you brought it out in me."

His eyes flashed desire as his finger brushed her nipple through the fabric, and it hardened instantly. "Then we bring out the best in each other, mate. As it should be. I always told you we were meant to be together."

He *had* always insisted that, even when she hadn't been so sure, and everything seemed stacked against them. Torven had known he wanted her—and that they would be perfect for each other—in a way that made her catch her breath. It was hard to resist a guy who looked at you the way he looked at her.

Trista glanced around. Luckily, the hangar bay wasn't busy since it was early in the artificially created space station day cycle. That didn't mean it was empty. A handful of aliens were inspecting ships, and a few Drexian pilots were preparing for departure.

"Torven." She bit her bottom lip as he flicked her nipple. "We can't."

"Oh, we most certainly can. If I cannot get my fill of you when I wake up, then I must get it here."

She sucked in her breath as he pinched her lightly. "On the hangar deck?" Part of her was horrified, and another part of her—perhaps a bigger part of her—was thrilled.

He pulled his hand out of her coveralls, and led her around to the other side of the ship. This particular ship happened to be docked at the far end of the high-ceilinged space, so there was nothing on the other side except for a curved wall.

"Better?" he asked, proceeding to unfasten the coveralls and tug them so that they dropped to her ankles. His mouth gaped when he saw what she had on underneath—the blue shorty pajama set she'd been wearing when they went to bed the night before. "You walked around the station in this?"

"Like you said, it was the middle of the night," she told him with a half smile. "No one was around to see me."

He continued to stare in disbelief. "Anyone could have seen your nipples poking through the thin fabric." His gaze lowered and his eyes widened. "And you aren't wearing any panties underneath these tiny shorts."

Her cheeks heated. "Like I said, I was in a rush." She darted a glance at her full breasts. "And my nipples weren't hard then."

"No?" He cupped her breasts in his large palms, thumbing the erect nipples. "This is all for me?"

"Of course, it's all for you." She lowered her voice. "You know that."

"Mmm." He closed the distance between them. "I like to hear you say it."

She met his gaze. "I'm only yours."

With a growl, he kissed her hard. Trista let the force of it press her back against the hull of the ship, wrapping her arms around his back and pulling him closer. She couldn't stop a small moan escaping as his tongue found hers, caressing urgently while continuing to thumb her nipples.

After a few moments, he slipped one hand from her breast and slid it underneath the waistband of her shorts. Using two fingers, her parted her slick folds and quickly found her clit. Her knees almost buckled as he began circling it with the tip of one finger.

"You're so wet for me, my little grease monkey," he whispered in her ear.

She couldn't speak as he dropped down, capturing one nipple in his mouth and sucking. Blood pounded in her ears as competing sensations of pleasure made her bite her bottom lip to keep from crying out. She didn't even care that they were in public, and anyone might walk around the ship and see them. As it was, it wouldn't take a genius to figure things out by looking at their legs underneath the ship, especially with her coveralls around her ankles.

"You taste so good," he said, pulling away from her nipple.

"Don't stop," she gasped.

He grinned up at her. "Where do want my mouth, Trista?"

Her breath caught in her throat, and she felt a spasm between her legs. "You know where I want it."

"Tell me," he said. "Tell me where to lick you."

Her cheeks burned. "My pussy. I want you to lick my pussy."

Dropping to his knees, he yanked her shorts down until they joined the coveralls on the floor. He teased a kiss on her thigh. "This tight, wet pussy?"

"Torven," she begged, stepping out of the clothes pooled at her feet and kicking them away.

He dragged his tongue between her folds, and she clutched at his shoulders so she wouldn't fall. It was almost too much as he began swirling his tongue over her clit, and when he lifted one of her legs, hooking it over his shoulder, Trista dug her fingers into his flesh.

His tongue continued to swirl while he slid a long, thick finger inside her, and began pumping it in and out. She dropped her head back, her eyes rolling up to the ceiling as her mate pleasured her, her heart racing and her hands gripping his shoulders so she wouldn't collapse. When he quickened his pace, she couldn't hold back anymore as her body convulsed around him, her release sending her catapulting over the edge. Clawing at his back, she gasped as wave after euphoric wave crashed over her.

She felt boneless when he stood and gave her a satisfied grin. As the hum in her head cleared, and her heart rate started to return to normal, she reached for him. "What about you?"

"As much as I would love to bend you over this ship and show you how wild you make me, I think they've probably waited long enough."

"Who's waited long enough?"

"Mandy and the other tributes." He reached down and retrieved her shorts. "That's actually why I came looking for you. They stopped by the suite to remind you about the party planning session."

Trista smacked her forehead and snatched the shorts from him. "Shit! The Christmas party. I totally forgot."

"I'm sure they'll understand."

She hopped on one leg as she pulled on the shorts. "You don't know Mandy. If I miss the meeting, I'll get stuck working with Serge on color-coordinating streamers, or something else ridiculous."

Torven handed her the coveralls with a grin. "I still don't understand this Christmas thing."

She stepped into the baggy suit and paused. "It used to be my favorite time of the year. I had a couple that weren't so great, but there was something about hearing Christmas music and seeing lights on people's houses that could always make me smile."

Torven tilted his head at her. "Lights on houses?"

She fastened the coveralls and took a deep breath. "Even in some of the crappiest neighborhoods—and I lived in a bunch—people would put little string lights around the edges of their houses. Sometimes they blinked. Sometimes they didn't. Some people only do white and some people are all about color. Honestly, I liked them all."

"Humans continue to fascinate me."

"Good thing for me." Trista gave him a quick kiss before she backed away "Now wish me luck that Mandy doesn't kill me."

CHAPTER
SIX

Ella leaned back on the transparent chair in the design studio, rubbing the crick in her neck as she spotted her best friend True walking across the chic, high-ceilinged space, her shoes tapping on the hardwood floor. "You're early."

The woman shook her head and her long, blonde hair swung behind her. "Actually, I'm not. You just lost track of time again. How long have you been staring at the screen?"

Ella glanced down at the tablet. "No idea. Has it really been that long? I feel like I just got to Preston's."

True sat down on another clear, wingback chair across from Ella, grinning at her friend. "Tell me something I don't know. As soon as you start working, the world disappears around you."

Sighing, Ella ran a hand through her mass of dark curls. Her friend was right. It felt like she'd just arrived at the floral design studio where she worked as a holographic programmer, but she vaguely remembered her boss, Preston, saying something about going out for lunch, and that had been a while ago. "At least it isn't as bad as when I was working on the military stuff. I definitely put in longer hours then."

"Do you miss it?"

Ella reached for her almost-empty coffee tumbler and swirled the contents so she wouldn't swallow a mouthful of dregs. "You mean, do I miss staring at data for hours, and worrying about making a mistake that might cost lives?"

True shrugged. "It must be hard to go back to creating holographic wedding designs after working on a top-secret project that ended up rescuing a captured Drexian."

"You know I love working for Preston." She knew that wasn't really an answer, but she didn't want to admit how much she missed working on military intelligence with a bunch of badass Drexian warriors. As much as she enjoyed working for the human designer, creating holographic sunsets and meteor showers for weddings wasn't quite as rewarding as saving lives.

True looked at her like she didn't believe her, reminding Ella that the woman knew her pretty well, which meant she also knew when she was trying to fool herself. But it wasn't like the Drexians were going to bring her onto their team permanently. She'd known the gig was temporary when she'd accepted it, and she'd been okay with that. Mostly.

"Even if the military needed me again, I couldn't abandon Preston," Ella said, blinking as she looked around the studio—all exposed brick and modern furniture that looked more like a New York City loft than part of an alien space station. "Not when we're about to get an influx of tribute brides."

True twirled a strand of pale hair around one finger. "Speaking of tributes, I'm not sure why you want me at this meeting. Everyone else is a tribute bride, right?"

"Not everyone. Shreya's another independent. Besides, the tributes aren't so bad once you get to know them." Ella took a sip of her now-cold coffee equivalent, wishing for the hundredth time that the Boat had real coffee.

True cocked an eyebrow. "Someone's changed their tune. You used to be pretty dismissive of the whole concept of tribute brides, and all the Earth women who went along with it."

Ella's cheeks flushed and her gaze dropped to her tablet.

"Of course, that was before you fell for your own Drexian warrior." True craned her neck, as if looking for someone. "I'm surprised he isn't here."

"Here?" Ella laughed. "I don't think Dakar wants to sit in on a meeting of tributes to plan a Christmas party."

True's face brightened. "I do love the idea of celebrating Christmas. The party we tried to do in the independent section last year wasn't great."

"It wasn't bad," Ella said, tapping her tablet's screen. "But we didn't have access to Drexian resources or technology. Now we do."

"And they're really letting you use the holographic tech to create a giant Christmas tree in the promenade?" True cast a quick glance over her shoulder at the door she'd entered from, beyond which was the promenade—the hub of the station.

Ella's brow furrowed. "I just have to figure out how tall I can make it without interfering with the inclinators. You know they move using magnetic force."

True gave her friend a sideways glance. "And why would I know that?"

Ella sighed. "It wouldn't kill you to learn more about the Drexian tech, True. It's pretty amazing, and you do enjoy using it, especially since I used my connections to get you time on the fancy officer holodecks."

True's pale cheeks colored. "Oh. I meant to mention...thanks for the addition to my holodeck program."

"Your holodeck program?" Ella ran a hand through her wild mane of dark curls. "What do you—?"

"Don't kill me for being late!" The door flew open, and Mandy bustled inside, breathing heavily. Her chestnut-brown hair was pulled up into a ponytail, with damp tendrils curling around the nape of her neck. One arm was looped through Bridget's, although the other woman didn't seem nearly as harried.

"I told you we wouldn't be the last ones," Bridget said, shaking her head as she was propelled across the room.

Mandy took in the space and Ella and True sitting around the low, clear table. "Where is everyone?"

Ella leaned back and crossed her legs. "Should we be offended by that, True?"

"You know what I mean," Mandy said with a flutter of her hand. "Katie and Trista are supposed to be here, too."

"And you asked Shreya to join us," Ella reminded her. "Although she's coming from the lab, so she may be late."

Bridget glanced over at Mandy, as the two took seats between Ella and True. "You're dragging Shreya from her research to plan a party?"

Mandy ignored her friend as she absently rubbed her swollen belly. "This isn't just any party. It will be the first official, station-wide holiday party. It should be amazing."

Bridget flicked the tips of her fingers through her straight, black hair. "Can it be amazing without stressing us all out? I'd like to enjoy my first Christmas on the Boat."

"I love the idea of a Christmas party," True said with a shy smile. "It's my favorite holiday."

"See?" Mandy gave Bridget a pointed look and beamed at True. "*Some* people are in the holiday spirit already."

Bridget folded her arms over her chest and peered down her nose at Mandy. "Excuse me? I'm in the holiday spirit, thank you very much. If I wasn't, would I have convinced Kax to play Santa Claus?"

Mandy's mouth hung open. "You did?"

Bridget fluttered her eyelashes and nodded. "I told you I would help."

"He must be seriously crazy for you." Mandy pulled a tablet out of her hot-pink tote bag and flipped it open. "I can't wait until Dorn sees him in a white beard."

"Kax still needs some elves, if Dorn is jealous he doesn't get to dress up," Bridget said.

Mandy stifled a laugh. "Somehow I don't think my hulking mate would make a very convincing elf." She tapped a finger to her chin. "Now Serge, on the other hand..."

"Would murder you," Trista said, as she and Katie walked in.

Ella couldn't help smiling at the blonde in stained coveralls. Trista didn't fit the usual image of a tribute bride, and since she'd returned from being stranded on an ice planet, she also didn't seem to care. Ella liked that the woman's hair was pulled up in a messy ponytail—and not for stylish effect—and that she made no secret of her love for mechanics. A woman after her own heart, she thought.

Mandy twisted around to look at the approaching women. "You don't think we could tell him the elf suit was the latest fashion on Earth?"

Katie gave a snort of laughter as she sat down on the upholstered bench. "I think the jingle bell shoes would tip him off. I, for one, don't want to get on his bad side again. He's barely forgiven me for having a surprise wedding without telling him."

"Too bad," Mandy said. "I think our wedding planner would make the perfect elf."

Bridget shook her head. "Why don't we let Ella tell us what she's come up with for the party, and then we can work from there?"

Ella spun her tablet around and swiped her fingers across the surface. "I think you'll like this. I thought we could do a giant Christmas tree in the promenade, and officially light it sometime during the party. I'll have the lights turn on from the bottom and spiral around the tree until they reach the star at the top, then holographic fireworks will go off above it. I'd really like for it to start snowing after that, but since the promenade isn't actually a holodeck, it won't feel like snow."

"You can do that? Make it look like it's snowing?" Bridget asked, her dark eyes widening.

"It's not hard." Ella's cheeks warmed, as all the women stared at her.

"Don't let her fool you," True said. "She's really talented when it comes to computers and coding."

"That's perfect," Mandy said. "So, we have a tree and snowfall. That will definitely set the scene. Then we have Kax as Santa, and possibly Serge as an elf."

Everyone rolled their eyes and laughed. As the women began telling Mandy again why tricking Serge into being an elf would be a bad idea, Ella heard a noise behind her. She craned her neck to see Dakar's head poking out from the doorway in the back of the studio. What was he doing here?

Luckily, the women were so caught up in the debate that they didn't do much more than nod when she excused herself and hurried to the back. Ducking through the doorway, she didn't have time to ask her mate what he was doing before he had her back flattened to the wall.

"I had to see you," he said, lifting her arms so they were pinned over her head and pressing his body to hers.

Ella's pulse quickened as he nuzzled his head in her neck, his breath warm and his scratchy stubble sending a frisson of excitement down her spine. "Are you insane?"

He shook his head as he murmured into her ear, "No Inferno Force warrior can be insane. They monitor us for signs of derangement."

She almost laughed. "I mean for coming here when I'm meeting with a roomful of tribute brides."

Dakar pulled back, his teal eyes flashing with intensity. "Don't you like the thought of them in the next room?" He kept one hand tight over her wrists while he moved the other down to cup one of her breasts, thumbing her nipple through the fabric of her button-down shirt. "Any of them could walk back here and see what I'm doing to you."

Heat pulsed between her legs, and she arched into him. "What are you doing to me?"

He kissed her deeply, his tongue parting her lips and stroking hers before he emitted a dominant growl, spinning her around so that she faced the exposed brick wall. With one hand, he deftly undid the front of her snug, black pants from behind and jerked them down below her hips. Leaning so that his body was flush against hers, he whispered into her ear. "I'm taking what's mine."

Ella could feel his hard length, and she ground her ass into him. "You think this is yours?"

"Mmhmm." He grasped her by the hips and tipped her ass up, then rubbed his palm over one ass cheek. "Your perfect breasts, this round ass." He gave her a sharp slap. "I know it is."

She bit her bottom lip to keep from yelping. Luckily, the women in the next room were talking loudly and hadn't heard the slap of flesh against flesh. Hearing their voices and knowing they were only steps away ignited liquid heat between her legs.

Dakar gave a rough tug at her lace panties, pushing them to the side before pulling his own pants down and dragging the crown of his cock through her hot folds. "All mine."

Before she could tell him what an arrogant ass he was, he'd driven into her in a single hard thrust, holding himself deep.

Ella splayed her hands on the rough brick to keep herself upright, her breath catching in her throat. Need stormed through her as she rocked back into him, bending forward and lifting her ass higher.

"You like this, don't you?" His words were a dark purr as he bent forward and nipped her ear. "You love taking my cock where anyone could see us."

He stroked into her again, and she swallowed her scream, her hips moving with him, needing more.

"Tell me you like it," he whispered, thrusting into her. "You want them to see how tight you're stretched around my cock."

Arousal nearly made her knees buckle, his desperate words sending shivers down her spine. He knew she liked the idea of being watched, the excitement of almost being caught with his huge cock pounding her so hard she could barely breathe. After being a good girl her entire life, she liked feeling naughty. The idea of being caught made her heart pound and her breath quicken.

He reached a hand around her waist, his fingers quickly finding her clit and circling it as he stroked in and out. "Tell me, Ella."

"I like it," she gasped, the sensations storming through her and eliminating all rational thought. She didn't care about anything but the feel of his thick cock inside her and his fingers stroking her, as she teetered on the edge.

"I know you do, *cinnara*. You love me fucking you like this." He slapped her ass again before driving even deeper. "You love being a bad girl who needs to be punished."

His words shattered her. Ella bucked against him as her body rippled around his cock, squeezing again and again as she threw her head back. She could feel him knifing up, his hands going to her hips as he thrust hard. Hot pulses filled her as he came, and they finally both stopped moving, although he held himself snug inside her, his cock still hard and twitching.

She steadied her breathing, again noticing the voices from the other room. "How am supposed to go talk about Santa Claus and elves now?"

Dakar feathered a kiss to the back of her neck, spanking her once more. "Who said I was ready to let you go?"

CHAPTER
SEVEN

"Care to explain yourself, young lady?"

Shreya swallowed hard as she entered the studio and all the tribute brides turned. She quickly found the source of the voice, and saw Ella walking out from the back of the room, tucking in her shirt. She knew her friend was teasing, but her face still warmed.

"Sorry, everyone. I had to swing by the lab."

"You're still working there?" True asked, patting the empty chair next to her. "I thought your project would be over once you all rescued Vox."

Shreya ran a hand through her thick hair, pushing it off her shoulder as she sat. "I'm still monitoring him for any genetic anomalies or mutations that might be a result of the Kronock's splicing his DNA."

"Sounds hot," Mandy said with a wink.

Shreya's face heated. She still wasn't used to the teasing that seemed to be par for the course with the tribute brides. She guessed she shouldn't be embarrassed. It wasn't like she was the only human to fall for a huge alien. They'd all taken Drexian mates— each one more gorgeous and built than the last.

She was the only one who'd been taken to an alien bordello, though. That information probably wasn't a secret on the station, nor was the way she'd been dressed when she'd been brought back. Her heart beat a little faster when she thought of the diaphanous, skimpy dress she'd been wearing when Ella and the Drexians had found her. And her mouth went dry when she remembered Vox dressing her in it while she was strapped to an X-cross. After that, she shouldn't be embarrassed by much of anything, although she still blushed easily.

"It must be hot," a woman with straight, black hair said, appraising her with a grin.

"Give the poor girl a break, Bridge." The redhead leaned over and waved at her. "I'm Katie. My husband also went through some stuff with the Kronock, and had a pretty rough surgery. If you ever need to talk, I'm here."

"Thanks." Shreya's shoulders relaxed. She'd met most of the tributes before, but she was glad to be reminded of their names. Her gaze scanned the group.

Ella and True she knew, since they were independents like her; Mandy she'd met when Vox had been in the medical bay; she guessed Trista was the one in coveralls, since she'd heard the woman liked to tinker with Drexian space ships; and that meant the girl Katie called Bridge must be Bridget, the tribute who'd been kidnapped from the station by the Kronock and rescued by her now-mate.

"I haven't seen you much since you moved in with Vox in the officers' wing," True said. "How's it going?"

Shreya couldn't help smiling. "Good."

"What's it like being with an alien who's part cyborg?" Bridget asked. "Did they enhance anything other than his eye?"

Mandy swatted the other woman's leg. "You're terrible."

"What?" Bridget shrugged. "I'm sure we were all curious."

"Just the eye," Shreya said, glad her cheeks didn't flame again.

"Although, even that was removed. There's only a sliver of metal left along his temple."

"Now that we've settled that," Mandy said, "can we please get back to the party?"

"I hope you didn't start without us." The Gatazoid's voice carried from the door as he and Reina bustled inside, Serge's platform boots clip-clopping on the hard floor, while the tall Vexling hurried along beside him.

"I thought we weren't involving Serge until the very end," Katie muttered, her gaze darting around the circle of women.

Trista gave a resigned sigh. "It's impossible to keep anything from him."

"Maybe the party will distract him from the fact that I keep putting off wedding planning," Ella said, under her breath.

"Hardly, sweetie," Serge said when he reached them, flicking his gaze to Ella then away. "I'm just letting it slide because I've got so much to do between this party, and preparing for all the new tribute brides."

"I promise Dakar and I will focus on it soon," Ella said.

Serge fluttered a hand at her. "Talk does not cook rice."

Shreya had heard that the pint-sized alien liked to use colorful Earth expressions. She put her fingers to her mouth to keep from giggling.

Ella rolled her eyes. "I promise I'll set a date."

Serge made a noise in the back of his throat that indicated he clearly didn't believe her, but he turned to Shreya with a wide smile. "And how is my other independent bride today?"

Reina steepled her bony hands. "It's so exciting to have independents taking mates. This is a first, you know."

"But it doesn't have to be the last." Serge let his gaze fall to True, who shifted in her chair.

"Are we here to plan a party or matchmake?" Mandy said, her voice rising.

"I've spoken to Vivan in acquisitions." Reina's pale-gray cheeks suddenly looked pinker than usual. "He's going to help us source any items we might need from Earth."

Mandy tilted her head at the Vexling. "Vivan?"

Reina let out a series of nervous titters. "He's a fellow Vexling from the same village as my family."

Bridget leaned forward and rested her elbows on her knees. "You don't say?"

"Get yourself together, Reina." Serge let out an impatient huff as he shot a look at the clearly flustered alien. "We don't have time for your silly infatuation."

"Hold on," Katie said. "I want to know more about this Vivan."

"Does this have to do with your former life as a reporter?" Serge asked, the roots of his purple hair slowly turning pink.

"I was actually more of a paparazzo, but I appreciate the bump in status." Katie swung her attention back to Reina. "What's the story with Vivan?"

"Nothing," Reina said, avoiding Serge's stare. "He's just very helpful when I need special items for my brides."

The women exchanged glances and knowing nods.

"Now if we're done with that, can we get back to the party?" Serge pulled a tablet from under his arm and his fingers danced across the surface. "I've done some research on Christmas food. I have to admit that it's a bit odd. The text I found doesn't mention what's in Who-pudding, and I'm afraid to ask about roast beast."

The women stared at him.

"Did you get all your information from *How the Grinch Stole Christmas*?" Katie asked.

Serge pulled himself up to his full height, which meant he was still only at eye level with the seated women. "Our R & D department said it was the most popular holiday reference book."

"I think we've determined that the R & D department needs to update their R," Mandy said. "I was thinking we'd do all finger foods for the party. Things that are easy to eat while people—and aliens—mingle."

"Mini quiche, baked brie, a cheese ball, pigs in blankets," Bridget added.

Reina inhaled sharply, although her cheeks had returned to their normal pale shade. "You eat pigs in blankets?"

"How barbaric and bizarre," Serge said, shaking his head. "And humans think the idea of aliens is crazy."

"They aren't real pigs," True said. "They're made with hot dogs."

"Dogs? Even worse!" Reina said, staggering to an empty chair. "I think I need to sit down."

"Why don't I get recipes to give to the chefs?" Mandy said. "The most important part will be the drinks, anyway. We want lots of bubbly, and maybe hot cider."

"And eggnog," Trista added, rubbing her stomach as Reina made a horrified face.

Shreya hadn't grown up celebrating Christmas, but she'd always liked the festive holiday. She could do without the madness of pumpkin-spice season and she'd never lived in the States to celebrate their Thanksgiving, but she did love hot apple cider, and the smell of cinnamon that seemed to fill the air in December. "And cookies. Lots of Christmas cookies."

"Yes," True beamed at her. "Maybe we could have a cookie-decorating station."

"I love that," Mandy said, clapping her hands.

"Can we sing carols at some point?" Bridget asked. "After everyone sits on my husband's lap and tells them what they want, of course."

Reina's large eyes widened. "Oh, dear."

Trista patted her leg. "Kax is going to play Santa, and it's a tradition for people to sit on Santa's lap."

Reina expression relaxed. "Humans have such interesting traditions."

"So we have holiday food, hot cider, cookie decorating, caroling, Santa," Mandy said, her gaze falling on Katie. "Anything special you want at the party?"

Katie shook her head quickly. "Nope. That should cover it."

Shreya wondered if Katie hadn't celebrated Christmas, either. She knew not everyone in the U.S. did. She felt her communication device vibrate in her pocket and dug it out, glancing at the readout. Her heartbeat quickened and she stood quickly. "I'll be right back."

She rushed out of the studio, pausing when she'd reached the shimmering, stone walkway of the promenade. Glancing around, she scoured the area for signs of Vox. He'd said he was outside, and that it was important. Was he experiencing side effects from the surgery that removed his cybernetic implant? Was he having more pains in his head?

She yelped when she felt strong arms wrap around her waist from behind. She twisted around to look up at him. "Are you okay?"

He lowered his mouth to her neck and kissed her gently. "I am now."

She turned to face him. "Don't tell me you called me out of a meeting for a kiss."

He gave a slow shake of his head. "Not just one kiss." He captured her mouth with his before she could protest, his lips warm and soft as they moved against hers.

Shreya let herself sink into the kiss, moaning when he parted her lips with a hard sweep of his tongue and deepened the kiss. Her arms went instinctively around his neck, as his tongue caressed hers. When he finally pulled away, they were both breathing heavy, and she felt lightheaded.

"I will let you get back to your meeting," he said.

"I should knee you in the balls again."

One eyebrow quirked up. "I hope you do not. That wasn't a pleasant experience."

She thought about her attempts to escape from him when he'd held her captive. "Neither was you tying me up."

Vox brushed a strand of hair off her forehead. "Oh, I don't know about that. The way your body reacted, I think you actually enjoyed it."

Her face heated at the memory. "You're begging to be slapped."

Bending his head so his lips brushed her ear, he whispered, "And you're begging for me to tie you up again, aren't you?"

Shreya opened her mouth to argue, but Vox nipped one earlobe quickly before stepping back. He gave her a wicked grin then turned and walked away.

"You bloody bastard," she muttered to herself, admiring the view as she watched him cross the promenade and disappear into an inclinator compartment. Her pulse was racing and her panties were wet. She hated to admit how right he was.

EIGHT

One week later

Reina bustled down the corridor toward the promenade, her arms laden with boxes and bags. She'd spent the past week not only working with the Earth women to pull together the holiday party, but also trying to decide the perfect gifts to get for everyone. Now that the party was in a matter of hours, she felt like a bundle of nerves. Would the party feel Christmasy enough for the tribute brides on the station? Would they like the presents she'd selected for them? Would Vivan actually come to the party?

The last thought made her heart flutter. Ever since the fellow Vexling had arrived on the station a year ago, she'd had a hard time keeping her mind off him. She wasn't sure if it was the wider set of his jaw or the luminous quality of his gold eyes, but he'd always struck her as one of the most handsome males of her species. The humans may be attracted to the bulky Drexians, but she preferred lanky limbs and long necks. Reina wished she had a free hand with which to fan herself as mental images of Vivan made her cheeks burn.

"At last!" Serge's voice jerked her from her thoughts and pulled her back to reality, as she entered the promenade and saw him perched on a ladder holding a digital megaphone to his mouth as he directed the party setup. "Presents under the tree, Reina. Chop, chop! No time to waste!"

She noticed the equally small Perogling, Cerise, holding the base of Serge's ladder, her curly pink wig reaching almost to the top step where Serge teetered. Cerise had arrived on the station with Shreya, after helping the human escape from a particularly dangerous planet. Now she lived in the independent section of the Boat, and shadowed Serge. Reina had welcomed her as an addition to their team because the high-strung Gatazoid now spent more of his time giving lengthy instruction to his mentee and less time worrying out loud to her.

Hurrying forward, Reina dodged Gatazoids setting out elaborate trays of food on long tables, and brown-horned Neebix in snug pants pushing levitating carts of glassware toward the bars. Without a free hand, she could only incline her head at Mandy, who stood next to Ella, appraising the towering tree that rose several stories into the air and was draped in swags of red ribbon and sparkling, gold balls. Piles of colorfully wrapped boxes already circled the base of the tree, and Reina tucked her armload of presents in with the rest.

"Isn't it amazing?" Mandy asked, walking over to Reina at the base of the Christmas tree. "Ella had to set up special holographic emitters on the promenade just so we could create a tree this large."

Reina knew that it had been impossible to bring a live tree from Earth, much to the dismay of the humans. Not only did the Drexians not relish the idea of tracking down and cutting a tree on Earth, their transport ships were not large enough to bring a thirty-foot tall, spiky tree. Luckily, Ella was skilled enough with holographic programming to create a convincing version. It even smelled like pine. Or at least, that was what they told her, to explain the sharp scent that made her nose twitch.

"Are all Christmas trees on Earth this large?" she asked, tipping her head back to see the star on top.

Mandy laughed. "Not even close. Most trees have to fit in people's living rooms, so they're about six or seven feet tall. Ella went all-out on this one."

Reina scanned the open-air space. The shops that lined the walkway were closed, and the café tables that usually clustered outside them were now draped in shimmering, green cloth, and topped with arrangements of red flowers. The potted trees had been draped in sparkly garland, and even the central fountain had been decked out, the cherub rising up from the center now wearing a red-and-green wreath around his neck. Even though Reina had no personal connection to the Christmas the humans loved so much, she had to admit that the decor made everything feel more festive and party-like.

"Looking for Vivan?" Mandy asked, in a furtive voice.

Reina blinked a few times. She hadn't been, but the mention of his name made her heartbeat quicken. "Vivan?"

Mandy nudged her. "Come on, Reina. It's obvious you like the guy. Every time we've mentioned him over the past week, your face has done exactly what it's doing now."

Reina pressed her fingers to her cheeks. "What is it doing?"

"Well, it has color in it for one. That's unusual. And your pupils are dilated. I don't know about Vexlings, but in humans that's a major sign."

Reina gave a quick shake of her head. "Vivan and I are old family friends. That's all."

Mandy raised an eyebrow. "Are Vexlings on the station allowed to date?"

"Yes, I suppose so." There was no rule against it, although there were far fewer male Vexlings than females. Since their planet had been nearly destroyed, their species had fewer males in general.

"Good." Mandy squeezed her arm. "I'd hate for us to be the cause of you getting in trouble."

Reina fluttered her fingers at her throat. "Why would you get me in trouble?"

"Christmas is a time for family and togetherness and love. Not that my Christmases growing up were like that, but that's what it's supposed to be." Mandy rubbed a hand across her belly and smiled. "Maybe it's because I'm crazy in love myself, or maybe it's the pregnancy hormones, but I want everyone to be as happy as I am. And even though this is an alien space station, I want this to be the best Christmas ever. For everyone."

Reina looked at the tribute bride. She did seem to glow with happiness, but she wasn't sure what the woman was going on about.

"Like they say in *Love, Actually,* which is the best holiday movie ever, by the way," Mandy continued, "if you can't say it at Christmas when can you say it?"

"Say what, dear?" Reina asked, wondering if she should check the tribute for a fever.

"That you like Vivan, of course!" Mandy beamed at her. "Before the end of the party, the girls and I are going to make sure that you get your happy ending, too."

Reina swallowed hard, her heart hammering in her chest as Mandy flitted away to talk with Dorn. This Christmas thing was turning out to be more complicated than she'd expected.

CHAPTER
NINE

Mandy gave Reina one final smile over her shoulder, leaving her to join Dorn near Santa's workshop on the other side of the enormous Christmas tree. He stood in his dark Drexian uniform, the sash with his commendations and medals draped across one shoulder, with his arms folded over his broad chest. He stared at the brightly colored backdrop for the ornate chair.

She slipped an arm around his waist. "What do you think?"

His shoulders relaxed as he wrapped an arm around her, the corner of his mouth twitching up. "This is where Kax will sit when he is dressed as the fat man in red?"

"Santa," Mandy corrected him for, what she was sure was, the hundredth time. She was also sure that Dorn did it on purpose each time. "And yes. People can come sit on Santa's lap and tell them what they want."

Dorn's hint of a smile became a full-blown grin. "This I am looking forward to."

Mandy swatted his chest, which was so hard and muscular she knew he'd barely felt it. "Be nice, or I'll make you take a turn as Santa."

The smile vanished. "You wouldn't."

She arched an eyebrow at him. "Wouldn't I?"

Her mate groaned. "You are an impossible female." He pulled her tighter. "Good thing you are mine."

"Oh, yeah?" She wiggled closer to him. Back on Earth, she would have freaked if a guy had called her "his," but now she loved when Dorn claimed her. She knew that Drexians mated for life, and the thought that this hot, hunky, ass-kicking warrior wanted no one else but her made her pulse quicken. The idea of being mated to an alien may have taken some getting used to—especially an alpha who was used to getting his way like Dorn—but now she couldn't imagine anything better than Dorn calling her his.

He nodded, raking a hand through the dark, shaggy hair that curled around the nape of his neck. "You need someone who can keep you under control." He moved his other hand down to the curve of her ass, tapping it sharply.

Mandy's core heated. She'd never been one to take orders, or fall in line easily before, but she loved when her mate got dominant. He made her feel delicate and feminine compared to his massive bulk —and his massive everything. Rubbing a hand over his chest, she let it drift south a few inches, and felt his impressive length harden against her hip. "What were you saying about control?"

"Minx," he said, his voice a low purr.

"Am I interrupting?" Dorn's brother's voice made them both look up.

Kax was not yet in his Santa suit. He also wore his Drexian military uniform, but where Dorn's hair was long and his face covered in scruff, his brother wore his hair short, and barely a day's worth of stubble on his cheeks. If they didn't both have eyes an identical shade of vivid green, it would have been hard to know they were related.

"Of course not." Dorn straightened, but did not drop his arm from around her waist. "I was merely inspecting your throne, big brother."

Kax rolled his eyes. "I do not know how my mate talked me into this."

Mandy thought of her best friend Bridget's lithe body and her toned, dancer's legs. She could guess pretty easily how he'd gotten suckered into it. "It will be great. Everyone will love it."

Kax grunted then turned to Dorn and stepped closer. "I wanted to talk to you before the party."

Dorn must have noticed the solemn tone his brother had taken. The teasing grin fell from his face. "What is it?"

Kax glanced around before continuing. "We were right about the Kronock. They aren't happy we took the hybrid cyborg from them."

Dorn shifted from one foot to the other. "They put a lot of time into him, and from what Vox said, he was key to their plan to invade Earth. I'm sure it was a big blow."

A Vexling with an armful of gold garland hurried by humming "All I Want for Christmas," and Mandy stepped to the side so he could pass.

Kax waited until the willowy alien was several feet away. "Some of my informants have reported increased Kronock activity."

"What kind of activity?" Dorn asked.

"They seem to be ramping up production of their new battleships."

Dorn scowled. "The ones with jump technology?"

Kax nodded. "Courtesy of our Drexian traitors. My spies also report chatter about a major attack."

"*Grek*," Dorn said, muttering the curse under his breath.

Mandy held up a hand. "Wait a second. Does this mean they're still going to attack Earth, even though you rescued Vox?"

"We don't know," Kax admitted. "We don't have anyone inside the Kronock empire, so all this is hearsay from aliens who do business with them. Luckily for us, the Kronock like to brag."

Mandy's mouth went dry. She'd seen the Kronock, up close and personal. If she thought the Drexian were badasses, the

Kronock were terrifying and ruthless. After surviving one attack by them—and almost losing Dorn—she had no desire to experience any more encounters with the scaly, alien monsters. Just thinking about their clawed limbs and gray scales made her shudder.

Dorn gave her a small squeeze. "Don't worry, *cinnara*. We won't let them destroy your home world."

Mandy gazed up at him and squeezed him back. She loved when he used the Drexian term of endearment. "I know you won't." She glanced at Kax. "Should we go ahead with the party?"

"Of course." He managed a smile. "None of the reports we've received noted an imminent threat. I suspect we have several rotations before they would make a move. I have a feeling they're still regrouping after losing Vox. It will take them some time to come up with another strategy, although this one may rely less on sophisticated science and more on brute force."

Dorn let out a breath. "That is their strength."

Mandy looked from one brother to the other. "But things just went back to normal. A new group of tribute brides recently arrived, from what Serge told me. Does this mean all that stops again?"

Kax's brows pinched together. "For a while at least. I've already talked to Captain Varden. He's going to place the station's defenses on high alert and increase our fighter patrols. When they come, we'll be ready."

Dorn gave his brother a sharp nod.

Mandy bit her lower lip and glanced around at the preparations for the party. It felt odd to be celebrating, when a vicious enemy might be making plans to destroy Earth and them. Then again, what was the point of surviving if you couldn't enjoy life a little? She ran a hand over her taut belly. She refused to let the possibility of something bad ruin her happiness. Being abducted, brought to the Boat, and being matched with Dorn had given her a second chance at life—a happy life—and she wasn't going to let a bunch of awful Kronock spoil that. Not today, at least.

She took a deep breath. "I'm going to go find Bridge. I think she was picking up your Santa suit from Monti and Randi."

Kax gave her a weak smile. "I'm not sure if I think that's worse news than the Kronock movement."

"Ha-ha." She slapped his arm playfully. "If nothing else, it will take your mind off things."

Dorn rocked back on his heels. "I know I won't be able to think of anything else."

Kax narrowed his eyes at his brother, then shifted his gaze over to Mandy. "Doesn't this Santa also give out lumps of coal? Does he ever use this coal as a projectile weapon?"

"No." Mandy laughed. "Santa is supposed to make people happy. Not wound them."

"Too bad," Kax grumbled.

Mandy slapped her mate on the ass as she stepped away, leveling a finger at both men. "It's Christmas. That means it's the season for being jolly. No more talk of alien invasion until after the holidays."

That's something she'd never thought she'd say, Mandy thought, as she left both men looking very out of place amid the merry decor and blinking lights. As she headed for the bridal salon they'd tasked with creating the Santa suit, she hoped her wish for Christmas would come true. Was it too much to hope for peace on Earth when she knew about the Kronock?

CHAPTER
TEN

Bridget eyed the red-and-white suit that the pair of alien dress designers held up for her inspection. She sat on one of the white, tufted chairs in the ornate shop, the crystal chandelier glittering overhead and sending prisms of light bouncing off the high ceiling. The walls of the shop that weren't lined with mirrors were covered in hanging gowns—mounds of fluffy white fabric billowing out from hangers. The Drexians had done an admirable job of making the bridal salon look like it might on Earth, aside from the levitating platform where brides could look at themselves from all angles as it rotated in mid-air.

The only things not feminine and frilly in the shop were the pair of aliens standing in front of her in black Nehru jackets that reached below their knees. She didn't know what species Monti and Randi were, but they looked surprisingly humanoid, except for their metallic hair—one gold and one silver—and the fact that they never blinked. Of course, she had no idea what other alien traits they could be hiding under their long jackets and skinny pants—a short tail, a spiked spine, gills? She shook the thought from her mind and took a tiny sip of her drink, flinching from the taste.

They'd insisted on handing her a glass of bubbly, even though she was no longer a bride shopping for a dress, and the pink alien drink literally bubbled up as she held the glass flute in one hand. Usually, she loved the alien version of champagne, but today the fruity scent made her stomach churn. The stress of the party planning must be getting to her, she thought.

"What do you think?" Monti asked, his voice chirpy.

Bridget set the glass down on a side table and smoothed her palms down the front of her forest-green cocktail dress. "The colors are perfect."

Monti beamed at Randi, who touched a hand to his spiky, gold hair and gave her a Cheshire-cat grin.

"I'm not sure about the sparkles," Bridget said, choosing her words carefully. She knew that the alien designers could be touchy about critique.

Randi waved a hand at the white border of the red jacket. "We know you said white fur, but it seemed so dull without a little bling."

The red jacket and pants were edged in rows of fluffy white fur —faux, she hoped—with a line of bugle beads embellishing the fluffy cuffs. It was hard to imagine her tall, muscular mate wearing something so sparkly.

Monti shifted and the beads knocked against each other. Or so noisy.

"Why don't we ask the Drexian himself?" Randi asked, looking past her toward the front door.

Kax ducked slightly as he entered the shop and a bell trilled overhead. He caught sight of Bridget and the two alien designers, and wound his way around elaborate display tables to reach them.

"We were just showing your mate the Santa suit," Monti said, his smile wide as he stared up at the tall, Drexian warrior.

Kax looked at the suit, and then peered down at Bridget with one eyebrow cocked. "This is what you wish me to wear?"

She stood and leaned against him, enjoying the solid feel of him and the warmth emanating from his body. "Not exactly." She dropped her voice. "This is a little more flashy than most Santas. Unless you're a drag queen."

His raised eyebrow went even higher. "I may be from one of the elite houses of the Drexian empire, but I am not a queen. We do not have royalty."

There wasn't time for her to explain drag queens. Bridget turned to Monti and Randi. "The suit is perfect, except we need to lose the beads."

Monti's face fell. "But that's the best part."

"It's our touch of creative expression," Randi said.

Bridget leaned close to the two men, putting her hand up to the side of her mouth as she whispered, "I don't think someone as straightlaced as Kax can pull it off."

They quickly glanced at the imposing Drexian, and away again.

"You might be right," Monti whispered back.

Randi bobbed his head up and down, giving her a sympathetic look. "I see what you mean. It does take a certain panache to pull off glitz."

Monti patted her hand. "We'll take them off. You two just wait right here." And, with that, the pair bustled off to the back of the shop, dragging the bulky red-and-white suit with them.

Kax pulled her close, wrapping his thick arms around her. "I don't know whether I should be thanking you for saving me from that sparkly outfit, or if I should still be upset that you roped me into this in the first place."

Bridget pressed her palms against the hard planes of his chest, tilting her head back to look up at him. "Once they get the suit fixed, you're going to be the sexiest Santa this side of Saturn."

He chuckled and ran a finger down the side of her face. "If you say so, although I cannot imagine a chubby elf with a white beard being sexy."

"Usually, I'd agree with you, but I don't think there's ever been a Santa as built as you." She moved one hand down from his chest to his stomach, her fingers bumping across the defined ridges of his muscles through the dark fabric of his uniform. "Or one with a six pack."

His brow furrowed. "Are you feeling better than you were this morning?"

She remembered the nerves she'd had when she'd woken up and realized that today was the day of the big party. Although she was used to performing on stage, party planning was something else altogether. Between Mandy's eagerness to make the station feel like Christmas, and Serge's general excitability, she definitely had butterflies.

"Much better," she assured him. As long as she steered clear of the bubbly.

He smiled, a low growl escaping from his throat, and he glanced around the empty shop. "How long do you think it will take them to fix the suit?"

Bridget grinned up at him, taking him by the hand and pulling him to the nearest dressing room. "Long enough, tough guy."

The dressing room was spacious, with a single upholstered chair and a three-sided mirror angled around the open space. Shiny hooks were bolted to the bare walls, and Bridget remembered using them to hang all the gowns she'd tried on back when she'd been planning her wedding to Kax.

Her pulse fluttered as she reminded herself that she was actually married to the gorgeous alien, whose hands were roaming up her thighs as he pushed her up against one of the walls that didn't have mirrors. Bridget used her foot to push the door of the dressing room shut behind them.

"I like your dress," he said, as he kissed her neck and ran his hands up under the short, flared skirt. His fingers found the wisp of lace that was her thong. "But I like this even more."

Bridget's breath caught in her throat as his fingers skimmed underneath the strip of lace, running down the curve of her ass to the slickness between her thighs. It took only the softest touch from him to get her wet, and she felt a rush of heat between her legs as his fingers teased her.

Lifting her face, Kax crushed his mouth to hers, his kiss hard and needy. Her moans were swallowed as his tongue delved deep, and desire arrowed through her. His touch felt hot on her flesh, and she instinctively arched into him, savoring the feel of his hardness.

Moving with desperate quickness, she unfastened his pants and yanked them down so they pooled to the floor. He groaned, deepening his kiss as she stroked him through the tight boxer briefs that could barely contain his swollen length. Slipping her fingers beneath the fabric, she freed his cock and wrapped one hand around the shaft, her fingers not reaching all the way around.

Pulling back, she met his molten gaze. "I need to taste you."

His eyes were half-lidded with desire as she led him to the chair and pushed him down, kneeling between his open knees. Bridget locked eyes with him as she took the crown of his cock in her mouth. The skin was velvety smooth, and she made a small breathy noise as she let her lips slide down and take him fully in her mouth.

Kax clutched the arms of the chair; letting out a primal sound when she sucked hard, then took his shaft into her throat. She couldn't take all of him. His cock was too long, and she fisted the base of it even as she felt the crown hit the back of her throat.

Moving her mouth up and down his rock-hard length, Bridget felt the slow burn between her own thighs and the electric tingle along her skin. She felt powerful hearing his moans and feeling him arch up beneath her, desperate to have more of his cock in her hot mouth. Arousal coursed through her and liquid heat coiled in her belly as she sucked harder.

With a single move, Kax lifted her up by the arms and brought her down on his cock, impaling her and making her throw her head back and gasp. The momentary shock as his thickness stretched her gave way to the intoxicating sensation of being filled completely. Bridget had never felt as perfectly complete as she did when her mate's cock was lodged deep.

Bridget met his gaze, his green eyes dark and intense, and the veins on his neck straining. Her legs straddled his thighs, and he clutched her waist to lift her up and down.

"So tight and wet," he said, his voice rough.

She leaned down so that her lips buzzed against his earlobe. "So huge and hard. Just like I like it."

A low rumble was his only response, as he lifted her up again and spun her around so that she faced away from him. Leaning forward a bit, she arched her back as he continued to pump her up and down on his cock. The new angle sent a jolt through her body, and she felt her release growing.

Kax slid his hands up past her waist to cup her breasts through her dress. Even through the fabric, Bridget's nipples were puckered into hard points. The feel of his fingertips rubbing against them made her cry out, wanting more. Her breath was ragged and her heart raced, keeping pace with his frantic rhythm.

When he thumbed her nipples hard, her body detonated, convulsing around him. She screamed as the sensations tore through her, feeling his thrusts become more urgent as he hammered hard, finally holding himself snug as he pulsed hot inside her.

Bridget sank back against him, swiping a strand of hair out of her face as aftershocks made her body twitch. His chest rose and fell, his breath uneven and warm on her neck.

Sliding his hands up to her belly, he tucked his face next to hers. "Is there something you want to tell me?"

She twisted slightly to meet his eyes. "Tell you?"

He rubbed one hand over the curve of her usually-flat stomach. "This is new."

She glanced down. He was right. She'd never had a stomach pooch before. She frowned and ran her own hand over it. She knew she hadn't been eating more than usual. Actually, she hadn't had much of an appetite lately. Everything she tasted had made her want to hurl. Her mouth went dry. It couldn't be.

She turned to face Kax completely. "I thought it was impossible for us to get pregnant."

"Improbable, *cinnara*," he said. "Not impossible."

Tears stung the backs of her eyes, and she knew instantly. "We're pregnant."

Kax nodded, his own eyes shining as he pulled her into him. Muffled cheers went up from outside the dressing room door.

Bridget laughed through her tears of joy. "I guess the Santa suit is ready."

"Take your time, sweeties," one of the alien designers called out. "We're so happy for you."

Kax shook his head, chuckling as Bridget sat up. "This is the best Christmas present I could ever imagine."

"Does it make up for the suit?" she asked, motioning to the door.

He kissed her softly, then wiped away a tear from the corner of her eye. "Definitely." He cupped a large palm over her belly. "This—and you—make everything worth it."

CHAPTER

ELEVEN

Dakar leaned back to take in the towering tree twinkling with lights. "You have to admit. The humans have outdone themselves."

His best friend Torven grunted in response. "I still do not understand the point."

The promenade had started to fill with people, as cheery music was piped overhead. Instead of the usual instrumental music playing on the station that Ella had assured him was hilariously outdated, a singer was crooning about seeing mommy kissing Santa Claus. Dakar wondered if this Earth holiday was kinkier than he'd been told.

Serge and Cerise bustled around in matching cherry-red suits as he directed Vexling waiters, while Neebix bartenders wearing lighted antler headbands passed out red and green cocktails from behind the bars. A Gatazoid with blue hair steered a hovering cart around them topped with trays of confections, the heady scent of sugar trailing after it.

"It's a party." Dakar laughed, running a hand through his hair and sweeping it up in a top knot. "You know, fun. Drinking, dancing, women."

Torven cut his eyes to him. "I do not dance, and I already have a woman, as do you."

Dakar sighed. "I know that, but that doesn't mean we can't enjoy ourselves with our mates." He scanned the crowd looking for Ella, his breath hitching when he spotted her near the tree. Even though he'd already thoroughly inspected every millimeter of her body, the sight of his mate's wild, dark curls spilling down her back never ceased to arouse him. Naked or clothed, he found her to be the sexiest female he'd ever laid eyes on.

Torven snorted with laughter next to him. "You've never been good at hiding your feelings when it comes to females."

Dakar wrenched his gaze away from Ella. "Can you blame me, Torv? She's perfect."

Torven thumped him on the back. "I'm glad to see that your infatuation hasn't waned. You've finally found a female who can hold your interest and keep you in line. There was a time when I didn't think that was possible."

"What can I say? I'd never been in love before I met Ella."

Torven grinned, clasping his hands behind his back. "I am happy for you, my friend."

"I'm happy for both of us," Dakar said. "Who would have imagined things would have ended up this way, when you and I were on our way to the Boat from our Inferno Force battleship?"

Torven glanced down at the illuminated patterns of blue light swirling on the floor. "Not me."

Dakar nudged him. "Speaking of our better halves, where is Trista? Down in the hangar bay?"

Torven gave him a half grin. "Not tonight. From what I understand, the party is not optional for any of Serge's tribute brides, but she was running late getting changed, so she sent me on ahead. She said if I watched her dress, we'd end up spending the whole night in our suite."

"That sounds about right." He'd barely seen his best friend for a solid week after the wedding ceremony, and more than a few times,

Torven had shown up for meetings with his clothes disheveled and his face flushed.

"Dorn doesn't look like he's in the party mood, either." Torven nodded toward their former Inferno Force commanding officer who stood looking down at his device with a scowl on his face.

Dakar had seen the Drexian huddled in intense conversation with his brother earlier in the evening, and he hoped it was nothing serious. It hadn't been long since they'd wrested Vox from the Kronock's control, and he knew there would be retribution from their enemy at some point. He hoped for the humans' sake, it wasn't tonight.

"Why don't you spend time with your mate while I talk to Dorn?" Torven said.

"You sure?" Dakar would much rather steal a few moments alone with Ella, than talk battle and military strategy with two gruff warriors, but he did not want to neglect his duty.

Torven took a step back. "If there's something you should know, I'll tell you."

Dakar watched the massive Drexian part the crowd on his way to Dorn, before turning and heading for Ella, who stood at the base of the imposing tree with her friend True, holding a tablet with one hand and tapping the surface with the other. He had to push through groups of unmated Drexian warriors as they stood talking and looking awkwardly around, and mated Drexian-human couples in various stages of embrace. As he saw one Drexian give his bride a playful spank on the ass, Dakar wondered how many drinks the warrior had polished off.

He came up behind Ella and slipped his arms around her. "I didn't think work was allowed at the party."

She jabbed an elbow in his gut as she spun around. "What the hell—? Oh, sorry, babe. I didn't know it was you."

"Who else would it be?" Dakar rubbed his ribs.

True put a hand to her mouth, clearly to stifle a laugh. "You're brave to sneak up on her when she's working. She gets in an 'Ella zone' and forgets anyone else exists."

Dakar had seen her in that zone before, so he knew what the blonde was talking about.

Ella touched a hand to his midsection, her expression apologetic. "It was instinct. Did I hurt you?"

Even though it *had* hurt, Dakar shook his head. "Of course not." He wound an arm around her and pulled her close. "Any chance you can take a break and actually enjoy the party?"

True nodded. "That's exactly what I was saying. Everything is perfect, so she should relax."

"So far," Ella said. "I don't know if the holographic fireworks and snow will actually work. I've never set up a holographic display like this outside one of the holodecks or holosuites."

True put a hand on her friend's arm. "It will work. You're a genius when it comes to holo design."

"I agree." Dakar bent down, swept a mass of curls off her shoulder, and kissed the side of her neck.

Ella managed a smile and leaned back into Dakar. "You're both biased."

"Just because you created the perfect man for my holodeck simulation?" True said, twirling a strand of hair around one finger. "Yep, pretty much. If you can do that, you can do anything."

Ella tilted her head at True. "Perfect man?"

"Just the people I was looking for," Mandy said, interrupting the conversation as she hurried up with Reina in tow. "Have any of you seen Bridget?"

Dakar tried not to gape at the tall Vexling who stood next to Mandy. She wore a skintight, black dress and heels with straps that crisscrossed up her spindly, bare legs. Her blue shock of hair had been curled and she wore heavy rouge on her usually pale, gray cheeks.

"I haven't," Ella said, also staring at the Vexling. "Wow, Reina. You look..."

"Amazing," True finished Ella's sentence for her. "I love that dress."

Mandy had to reach up to put a hand on Reina's shoulder. "Doesn't she look great? She let me give her a makeover earlier."

Both women smiled, and Dakar managed to close his mouth.

"I looked for Bridget at the bridal salon, but Monti and Randi insisted she wasn't there." Mandy nibbled her bottom lip. "I'd hoped to have Santa out already."

"I'm sure Kax is getting dressed," Dakar said. He'd heard that the former member of the High Command had been sweet-talked into dressing up in a costume for the party. Ella had explained the concept of Santa to him, but he still found it bizarre. How could humans believe *that* story and not think there was life outside their planet? Ella had told him that it was only the children who believed, but Santa and the Tooth Fairy made him seriously question humanity. A flying creature who took teeth? It was barbaric, if you asked him.

Reina peered easily over the women's heads, clearly searching for someone. Dakar knew women well enough to know that the Vexling was out to entice someone. He wondered who it was.

"If you see either of them, let me know, will you?" Mandy asked.

"I hope you're getting to enjoy the party," True said. "After all the hard work you put in."

Mandy let out a long breath and touched her belly. "I'd enjoy it more if I could have a cocktail, but I do *not* trust this potent alien booze. One sip of Noovian whiskey and my baby might come out with extra limbs. You know even one drink can damage a fetus?"

Dakar knew that Dorn's mate worked in the sick bay, so he wasn't surprised by her medical knowledge. He thought her assessment of the drinks—especially the ones being served at the party—was on point. He caught a glimpse of a Drexian warrior with a pale-haired human kissing him, both of her legs wrapped around his waist. Another human woman was making eyes at an unmated Drexian, her tongue licking her top lip and causing him to growl. He glanced over at the Neebix bartenders—mischievous aliens known for being handsome and horny. He'd be willing to bet all the credits he had to his name that the special holiday drinks contained Palaxian Pleasure Tonic.

True's eyes grew wide. "That's odd."

Dakar twisted his head to follow her gaze, seeing the back of Captain Varden as he talked with Dorn and Torven. "What?"

True shook her head. "Nothing. I thought I saw someone, but it's impossible."

Mandy sucked in a breath. "There they are, and they're coming out of the bridal salon. I knew Monti and Randi were lying to me."

Dakar pivoted slightly to see Bridget walking hand-in-hand with a broad-shouldered man wearing red pants, and a red jacket edged with white fur and cinched with a wide, black belt. Even though he had a fake beard and a red floppy hat, Dakar could tell it was Kax.

"Aren't you glad I didn't sign you up for that?" Ella whispered to him.

"I love you even more than I did before, if that's possible."

Mandy clapped her hands. "Now it's really Christmas." She took the Vexling's hand. "Come on, Reina. We still need to find your guy and get you both under the mistletoe."

Reina gave them all a desperate look as she disappeared into the crowd with Mandy.

"What's mistletoe?" Dakar asked Ella.

"A plant people hang over doorways at Christmas. If you find yourself underneath it with someone else, you're supposed to kiss them."

"Really?" He nuzzled her neck, inhaling the sweet scent of her hair. "Where can I get some of this mistletoe? I have quite a few places I'd like to hang it in our suite."

She twisted, capturing his mouth and giving him a hard kiss. "As if you've ever needed mistletoe."

CHAPTER
TWELVE

Torven rocked back on his heels, as he rubbed the smooth craktow tooth that dangled in the hollow of his throat. Feeling the cool surface and the familiar ridges calmed him, and right now he could use a bit of calm. "These reports came from Inferno Force?"

Dorn gave a curt nod, glancing at Captain Varden, who had joined the party to find them and bring further news of enemy incursion.

"An Inferno Force battleship was destroyed," Varden said, his own hands clasped behind his back and his icy-blue eyes flashing with controlled fury. "Most of the warriors were able to abandon ship before it blew, but we did suffer casualties."

Torven's free hand closed in a fist by his side, bile rising in his throat. As a member of the Drexian empire's most elite—and most ruthless—fighting force, he'd been in countless battles against the Kronock, and never had the brutal creatures bested them. Not like this. The thought both enraged and terrified him. "Where are the Kronock now?"

The muscles in Varden's jaw tightened. He scraped a hand through the silver hair at his temple. "They jumped away, but it's my belief the strike against Inferno Force was an attempt to weaken our defenses before a larger attack."

"On Earth?" Dorn asked, his voice a murderous rumble. "*Grek.* Is this the precursor to an invasion attempt?"

It had been decades since the Kronock had made a run at the planet, primarily because the Drexians had been guarding Earth and protecting it from the violent aliens. Up until now, Drexian technology had been far superior to their enemy's capabilities. But after a Drexian traitor had given both secrets and technology to the Kronock, the sides were not so unevenly matched. The creatures Torven had always considered stupid brutes had developed and evolved, as well, modifying their own biology to become more fearsome foes. All, it seemed, for the purpose of defeating the Drexians and finally taking Earth.

"What do we do?" Torven asked, fighting the urge to bolt from the promenade and jump on a fighter.

"I've increased the station's fighter patrols," the captain said. "I've also added a few warriors to monitor long-range sensors. Inferno Force is moving half their fleet closer to us. Now that the Kronock have jump technology, having our toughest fighters so far away doesn't make sense. But primarily, we watch."

"Agreed." Dorn let out a steady breath. "What we can't do is panic. The enemy may have done this to send us scrambling. We need to maintain order and routine."

Easier said than done, Torven thought. He frowned as a group of giggling tribute brides pushed past them, holding bubbling red drinks. "We're throwing a party while the enemy might be preparing to attack."

Varden clapped a hand on his arm. "There is something to be said for celebration, even if I do not understand these strange human customs. Especially if we may be in for some long battles. Trust me, you should take your happiness where you can find it."

Torven knew the captain was right. He and his fellow Inferno Force warriors were skilled at playing hard and fighting hard. It was the only way to stay sane when your life was constantly at risk.

"I will keep you both updated," Varden said, his eyes catching something over Torven's head and widening, as his words drifted off. "It looks like some of the independent humans are here, as well."

Torven turned to follow his gaze, but the only independent he saw was Ella's friend True, standing near Dakar and Ella at the base of the giant tree. He wondered how the captain recognized the shy blonde, or why he seemed surprised. Perhaps the Vexling in garish makeup that Mandy was propelling through the crowd startled him. The wild, blue curls atop her head were eye-popping.

As Torven's attention shifted away from the humans and Vexling, he spotted Trista exiting the inclinator alongside Katie. Although he found his mate attractive in the casual attire she preferred, and even the coveralls she wore while working on the hangar deck, Torven's mouth went dry when he saw the dress she had on. Gold and shimmery, the fabric draped from thin strings at her shoulders and dipped low to expose the top of her cleavage. Most of her legs were also bare, as the dress ended around mid-thigh. The wavy, blonde hair she usually let fall around her face was swept up off her neck, with only a few wispy tendrils escaping from the sides.

"Torven?" Dorn asked him. "Are you okay? You stopped breathing."

Clearing his throat, he attempted to wrest his gaze from his mate, but failed. She'd seen him and was walking toward him, and seeing her move in the dress that looked like liquid gold made all the blood in his body rush south.

"I believe we should let our Drexian brother enjoy the festivities," Varden said, amusement brimming in his voice.

Torven barely noticed the two men leaving him as Trista made her way through the crowd. When she reached him, her cheeks were flushed pink.

"You look..." He closed the distance between them and placed one hand on her hip.

She tipped her head back to meet his eyes, her own blue ones sparkling. "Thanks, big guy."

"Hi, Torven." Katie said, laughing as she stood beside them.

He jumped, startled to realize his mate's friend was with her. He'd been so focused on Trista, he hadn't noticed the redhead in the emerald-green dress walking beside her. "Apologies." He turned to her and gave a quick bow. "It is nice to see you again."

She grinned. "You, too." Craning her head to peer around the party, Katie said, "I'm going to leave you two and try to find Zayn. He usually hates crowds, but he promised me he'd be here."

Torven gave her another bow as she winked at Trista then melted into the crowd of people. He turned his attention back to his mate. "I've never seen you in something so...bright."

The color in her cheeks deepened. "Mandy and Bridget talked me into it. They said I had to wear a dress to the Christmas party." She smoothed a hand down the front. "Is it too much?"

He pulled her closer, swallowing hard as he looked down at the swell of her cleavage peeking out of the top of the dress. "No, it's perfect. You're perfect."

She pushed against him playfully. "I'm hardly perfect."

"You are to me." His cock throbbed as he ran a hand down her hip and imagined sliding the soft, shimmering fabric up over her round ass. "How long do we have to stay at this party, anyway?"

"I just got here," Trista said, pretending to sound outraged. "And it took Katie forever to get my hair up, so you are not dragging me back to our suite so soon. Besides, I'll hear it from Mandy if I slip out early."

Torven groaned, readjusting himself as his cock strained in his pants. "It may kill me if I don't get you naked soon."

Trista shook her head, but he knew she loved it when he told her how much he wanted her. "I'm sure you'll survive for a little longer. I thought Inferno Force guys were supposed to be the toughest, most badass warriors in the galaxy."

He leaned his head down close to her ear. "Unless it comes to burying my cock inside you. Then I am completely at the mercy of your tight, little—"

"Torv!" She pulled back, her eyes as round as her open mouth.

He saw the sharp outlines of her nipples through the fabric of her dress and it was all he could do not to thumb them through the shiny gold. "You are sure we cannot sneak out?"

Trista glanced over her shoulder. "Well, it is a holiday party, and it's kind of an office holiday party since you all work together."

"What is an office holiday party?"

"Honestly, I've never been to one, but they're kind of notorious on Earth for being either super boring, or the time where people get way too drunk and do really stupid things."

He tilted his head at her. "That does not sound enjoyable."

She took his hand in hers. "Unless the really stupid thing is getting it on in the middle of the party."

"By 'getting it on' do you mean...?"

Trista nodded as she stood up on tiptoes to peer over the crowd. "There must be a place nearby we can sneak off to without leaving the actual party."

His heart hammered in his chest as she tugged him through the throngs of people who now filled the promenade. Surely everyone around him could hear it, even though the conversation and laughter had swelled to a loud buzz.

They avoided Kax sitting on an oversized chair in his Santa suit and looking tortured as they maneuvered past entwined pairs of Drexian warriors and tribute brides, as well as groups of aliens who worked on the station—Vexlings, Gatzoids, Allurans—before skirting the base of the towering tree. Torven knew it was holographic, but the prickly branches felt real as they brushed against his arm. When Trista reached the back, wedging them between the branches and the wall, she stopped.

"No one can see us back here."

Torven didn't mention that the spiky tree was pressing into his back. He didn't care, as long as she didn't care that they were only steps away from hundreds of partygoers. Cupping her breasts in his hands, he rubbed her nipples and they tightened into even harder points.

She arched into him and moaned, the noise thankfully drowned out by the holiday music. He flicked the strings of her dress off her shoulders and pulled her dress down in one hard jerk, exposing her full breasts.

She gasped, her blue eyes darkening as she locked her gaze on his. "You like to be a bad boy, don't you?"

"Only with you." He spun her around so that her hands were splayed on the wall, reaching around to tweak one nipple as he slid her dress up over her ass with the other hand. He hesitated when he did not find any panties.

She twisted her head to look back at him, a wicked smile on her face. "I'm going commando."

"Commando?" What did the military term have to do with her being bare under her dress?

"It means I'm not wearing any underwear." She wet her bottom lip with her tongue. "Easy access."

Torven thought his cock might explode, all ability to think disappearing as his mate wiggled her ass underneath his hand. He growled as he dipped a finger between her thighs, his cock throbbing as he felt her slickness. "You're so wet for me. Does going commando arouse you?"

Her only answer was a moan.

He squeezed one breast gently as he teased her opening with his fingertip. "Even these feel bigger. Can they swell when you want to be fucked?"

"Not swell," she said through ragged breaths. "They get bigger if I'm expecting."

Torven stopped as he processed the word and its meaning.

"Expecting?" He spun her to face him, his hands going instinctively to her belly. "Are you carrying my child?"

Trista gazed up at him, smiling. "I think so. The past week I've been really queasy and my body is more sensitive. I wanted to wait until after the party to confirm it with a doctor, but I'm pretty sure."

A lump hardened in Torven's throat and his eyes stung. After everything that had happened, he'd hardly let himself hope for a child. It had been enough that they were together. But, now...

He dropped to his knees and showered her soft, round belly with kisses as she laughed.

"Weren't we in the middle of something?" she asked, tapping his shoulder. "I didn't go commando for nothing, you know."

"Not here." He stood, pulling her dress back up, and then capturing her mouth in his, savoring the sweetness of her as he kissed her deeply. His mate had never tasted or felt so good, and he was almost lightheaded when he finally pulled away.

Trista looked dazed, as well, but she squealed when he scooped her into his arms. "What are you doing?"

"Taking the mother of my child to our suite," he said, striding out from behind the tree and through the parting crowd. "And taking my time."

CHAPTER
THIRTEEN

Z ayn leaned against the wall in an alley between the bakery and bookstore, enjoying the fact that everyone else was so preoccupied, drinking colorful cocktails and sampling the food on the various stations set up down the walkway, that they didn't notice him tucked away down the dimly lit passageway.

He preferred it this way. Ever since he'd escaped capture from the Kronock, loud noises and crowds bothered him. He traced a finger over the scars slashing his forearms, a reminder of the torture he'd withstood while in enemy hands. At least he was no longer in a dank cell, with nothing to look forward to but pain and guilt. Well, the guilt he still had, but it was lessening. Thanks to Katie.

He surveyed the crowded space, looking for his mate. Usually, she was easy to spot, her mass of reddish-blonde curls making her noticeable in any gathering. She'd gotten ready for the party with Trista, so he was not sure what she would be wearing. Of course, he liked anything she wore, but his preference was for her to wear nothing. His pulse fluttered as he thought of her stretched out in their bed, her wild curls spilling across the sheets.

"Is there room in there for two?"

Zayn jerked his head up to see Vox, the recently rescued Drexian who'd been turned into a hybrid Kronock cyborg. The only trace of the warrior's ordeal was a slim arc of steel around one temple.

Stepping back, he waved an arm at the narrow alley. "Please."

"I need a break from the curious looks," Vox said, leaning against the other wall and taking a sip of his bubbling, red drink. "I thought if anyone would understand, it would be you."

Zayn gave a dark chuckle. "I do know what it's like to have an entire station look at you like you're a walking bomb. Of course, in my case, it was partially true."

"How long did it take for you to be fully accepted as a Drexian again?"

"Give it time. It's only been a couple of weeks." Zayn shifted from one foot to the other. "There are days I think I'll never feel like my old self again, but maybe that's not all bad. In my former life, I didn't have a human mate."

Vox nodded. "I might have gone mad if it hadn't been for Shreya."

"From what I hear, you'd be dead if it hadn't been for her."

"That is also true." Vox glanced out to the party, taking another big gulp from his glass. "Where is your tribute bride?"

Before Zayn could explain that she was on her way, he saw a flash of red hair in the crowd. "I think she's just arrived. You'll have to excuse me." He inclined his head at the Drexian, then cut his eyes to the warrior's drink. "Be careful with those. Either they're made with Palaxian Pleasure Tonic or everyone at the party is just extremely aroused."

He left Vox staring openmouthed at the drink and narrowed in on his mate, tracking her distinctive hair as she stood with Trista and Torven, then moved away. When he finally intercepted her and slid a hand around her waist, she jumped.

"I am sorry if I scared you," he said, not releasing his grip on her.

"You didn't scare me." The guarded look disappeared as she stepped closer to him. "I thought you might be one of these horny, unmatched Drexians."

"They would never lay a hand on you," he said, sweeping a dark look at the warriors around them.

"Maybe not under normal circumstances, but everyone here seems pretty loose and happy."

She was right. Aside from a number of mated couples wandering off to dark corners, even the unmated Drexians were eyeing unattached females—human and non-human—with barely disguised desire. When he'd spotted the Neebix behind the bars earlier, he'd suspected that there might be a problem. That species loved nothing more than stirring up drama, especially of the sexual nature, and were known to go heavy on the Palaxian Pleasure Tonic. He and Katie had fallen victim to the inhibition-loosening liquor once, although his memories of that evening made his heart beat faster and his throat go dry.

"Do you mind if we get out of here?" he asked.

Her brow furrowed in concern. "Are all the people—and aliens —freaking you out?"

"I'm fine, but I'd rather spend the evening alone with you than watching others embarrass themselves."

Katie laughed. "Then a holiday party is definitely not your scene." She slipped her small hand in his. "Christmas isn't my jam anyway. Let's blow this joint."

Although her words confused him, he was glad she was willing to leave early. He led her through the crowds, dodging a group of humans laughing and sloshing their drinks on the floor as they gestured with their hands. Serge passed them in a near-jog, muttering something about too many people making love by the garden gate and making a beeline for one of the bars as he wagged his finger at the Neebix bartender with the swishing tail.

Zayn pulled Katie with him onto an open inclinator compart-ment, releasing a breath when the doors shut and it surged upward. The pulsing, lavender glow and soft, instrumental music were a welcome respite after the pulsating music and swirling lights of the party.

When the doors opened again, they seemed to be on a different planet entirely. The teakwood path led across a holographic savannah, the tall grasses rustling as the moon shone over them. Even though Zayn had never seen a place like this in real life, the artificial environment now felt like home. He and Katie walked hand-in-hand down the familiar walkway—glancing over at the open-air bar and fire pit down a side path—their shoes tapping on the wood.

Zayn hesitated when he reached the doorway to their fantasy suite. He hoped she would like the surprise he'd planned for her. Ever since his mate had mentioned not having happy Christmases when she was growing up, he'd been determined to make this one different. He knew it couldn't be the same as being on Earth, but he'd worked with both Serge and Reina—and Reina's contact in the procurement division—to plan what he hoped would be a dream Christmas.

Waving his hand over the side panel, he held his breath as the door glided open. Luckily, Katie's early departure to get ready with Trista had given him ample time to set everything up, but that had been during daylight. Now that it was dark, he got the full effect.

Katie inhaled sharply, then glanced over at him. "Did you...?" She put a hand over her mouth as she stepped inside. "Is this for me?"

A tall, frosted tree took up most of the middle of the suite, with multicolored lights strung around it, and a glowing, gold star perched on top. Glittering balls and spun-glass icicles festooned the branches and wrapped presents were piled beneath. A replica of a fireplace stood to one side of the tree, with two knit stockings hanging from the mantle. A plate of iced cookies and two steaming mugs of hot cocoa—or at least, the Drexian version of it—sat on one of the suite's existing, safari-style tables.

"I wanted you to have a special Christmas," Zayn said, watching her. "I know it won't make up for all the bad ones, but I thought it could be a start."

"It's perfect," she whispered, her voice cracking. She threw her arms around him, burying her face in his chest.

He held her tight, only pulling away when he felt her body trembling. "Are you crying?"

"They're happy tears," she said, her eyes glittering as she looked up at him. "No one's ever done anything like this for me."

He brushed a finger across her wet cheeks. "You know I will do anything to make you happy."

Katie wrapped her arms around him again, and squeezed. "It's what I always imagined when I was little, but never actually got."

"Really?" Warmth spread throughout Zayn's chest as she held him, and he stroked a hand down her hair.

"Really, really." She stepped back, walking to the tree and touching one of the glass ornaments. "My dad was always too busy running cons to plan anything for Christmas, and we were always moving from place to place, so Christmas day was usually Hungry Man turkey dinners and some present he'd fleeced off someone. We never got a tree until they were all half dead and on sale, if then. A couple of times I made paper chains, but they never looked very good. Nothing like this. This looks like it could be in a movie."

Zayn joined her at the tree, which only stood about a foot taller than him, although the star brushed the top of the tented ceiling. "Serge assured me that a tree that was covered in fake snow was the latest in Christmas style."

Katie laughed, swiping at her eyes. "It's perfect, although I'm not sure how Serge considers himself an expert on Christmas."

"I believe Serge considers himself an expert in everything." He reached for a wrapped box under the tree and handed it to her. "Some of these boxes are just for effect, as Serge put it, but this present is for you."

She blinked at the silver box for a few seconds, before walking to the edge of the large bed, the sheer, fabric netting pulled back to the corners, and sitting down. She gingerly removed the bow and then peeled back the paper. "I always told myself that if I got a special present, I wouldn't rip the paper like some kids did. I'd enjoy opening it."

Zayn sat down next to her as she lifted the top off the box underneath the wrapping paper, his heart beating quickly in anticipation. He'd never selected a Christmas present for someone before, and he wanted so desperately for her to like it.

"Is this...?" She gaped at what was inside the box. "I can't believe you got me a camera!"

"I know you used one on Earth, so I had one of our procurement officers bring one back on the latest supply run." He studied her face. "Do you like it?"

"I love it." She lifted it from the box, turning it around in her hands. "And it's a really nice one."

Watching her face light with joy, Zayn realized he hadn't felt this happy in his entire life.

Katie set the camera down next to her and climbed into his lap. "Thank you, Zayn. This is by far the best Christmas I've ever had. And I love my present." She kissed him slowly, her tongue parting his lips and teasing the tip of his tongue. "But it's being with you that makes all of this perfect. I love you more than anything you could ever give me."

He nestled his face in her neck, inhaling the heady scent of her skin. "I feel the same way, *cinnara*. I don't need anything but you."

She wiggled out of his lap, tucking herself between his knees and unfastening his pants. She wet her lips as she gave him a wicked grin. "But you haven't gotten your present from me, yet."

Zayn leaned his head back as her mouth found his cock. Christmas was just as magical as the humans said it was.

CHAPTER
FOURTEEN

Shreya took a tall glass from the Neebix bartender, ignoring his brown horns that were flushed pink and the long tail that flicked behind him. One bit of advice she'd gotten not long after she'd arrived on the space station and decided to join the independent females had been to stay away from the Neebix, no matter how handsome and charming they might seem. It hadn't been a tough rule to follow since, before recently, she'd rarely left the independent section of the Boat, but she could see how one might succumb to their charms. The frisky aliens knew not to touch tribute brides, but that was about the only rule they followed. And even if they didn't touch, they certainly relished looking.

"Enjoying the party?" he asked with a smile, as he leaned over the bar. Between the Christmas carols being piped in overhead and the buzz of conversation, it was hard to hear or be heard.

She nodded, turning her back on him to put an end to the conversation and taking a gulp of the red cocktail, the sweet bubbles tickling her throat as she swallowed. She didn't want to give him the wrong idea. Shreya might not be a tribute bride, or officially mated to a Drexian yet, but she'd moved in with Vox, so in her mind, she was 100 percent his. Her heart quickened its pace as she thought about the Drexian with chocolate-brown hair and sea-green eyes. *Her* Drexian. Speaking of Vox, where was he?

Raising herself up on tiptoes, she attempted to see over the crowd. Not an easy feat, considering the fact she was so much shorter than every Drexian warrior, and a good deal of the other aliens and humans. She recognized the Drexian warrior Torven, with whom she'd worked to rescue Vox, snaking his way through the crowd with Trista. She almost did a double take at the blonde. It was the first time she'd seen the woman with her hair done up and wearing a dress.

Shreya glanced down at her own outfit—a long, red-and-gold paisley-patterned saree skirt with a cropped, snug-fitting choli top. It was her way of combining her heritage with the holiday season, although she felt a little out of place amid all the cocktail dresses and sparkly outfits. She'd pulled her thick, dark hair up on one side and let it cascade down the other shoulder in loose waves. It was a far cry from what she wore every day when she went to the lab, but the other women had insisted everyone dress up for the party. She tugged at the top that ended right under her ribcage and took another big gulp. It had been a long time since she'd shown this much skin in public.

"I almost didn't recognize you," the high-pitched voice said, pulling her attention down.

"Cerise!" Shreya smiled at the tiny alien with the towering, pink wig and the slightly iridescent blue skin. Officially, she was a Perogling who'd been given sanctuary on the Boat after providing assistance in the retrieval of Vox from the Kronock. Unofficially, she was the reason Shreya had escaped the lawless planet of Lymora III.

"I like this." Cerise bobbed her head up and down as she appraised Shreya's saree. "It's colorful. You look good in color."

"Thanks. You look nice, too." Even though Cerise had recently taken to shadowing Serge—and dressing like him—she had a fondness for frill. Her bright-red suit did not disappoint, with a row of fringe down each sleeve and a full, ruffled skirt.

"It's my first Christmas," Cerise said, her garishly painted eyes wide as she took in the surroundings. "I heard this Santa fellow has a long, white beard. I like beards."

Shreya leaned down so the small alien could hear her over the chatter. "Santa is just Kax dressed up in a special outfit. And a fake beard."

Cerise's face fell. "Carpithian testicles!"

Shreya assumed this was a Perogling curse. She laughed and drained the rest of her drink, feeling the warm buzz spreading all the way to her toes.

Cerise put her hands on her hips and sighed. "These Drexians are too hairless for my taste. I'd hoped this Santa fellow would be my type."

"Sorry," Shreya said, before changing the subject. "How are things going in the independent section?"

The smile returned to her friend's face. "Great. The humans are very nice."

Shreya accepted a fresh drink from the bartender, avoiding his gaze. "And work with Serge?"

"The new tribute brides have arrived already, but they're still being processed through the medical bay. Soon, we'll be assigned our humans and start planning their weddings. Serge is hoping one of the new crop of brides will want something over the top."

"I'm sure he is," Shreya muttered.

"That reminds me," Cerise tapped her chin with a stubby finger. "You and Vox haven't done much planning for your wedding, yet."

Shreya took a sip of her drink. "He's still adjusting to everything. We'll probably do something simple and intimate."

"I won't tell Serge," Cerise said, and then her expression brightened. "Speaking of your cybernetic mate..."

Shreya didn't correct her friend, and remind her that Vox was no longer part cyborg. The butterflies in her stomach made it hard for her to speak, as she watched the broad-shouldered Drexian cut his way through the crowd. His sea-green eyes darkened as he took her in, his gaze lingering on her exposed midriff.

"I'll see you both later," Cerise said, her skirt swinging as she moved away. "I want to get a good spot for the tree lighting ceremony, anyway."

Vox didn't seem to notice Cerise slipping into the crowd. He took Shreya's hand and brought it to his lips. "My beautiful mate."

Her cheeks warmed, the heat from his lips sending a shiver down her spine. "I thought maybe you'd decided not to come."

He shook his head. "And leave you alone? Never."

She glanced around the crowd, noticing a few curious stares at the metal remaining on Vox's face. "We don't have to stay."

Stepping closer to her so that their bodies were nearly flush, he touched a hand to her bare stomach. "And miss the tree lighting?"

She giggled. "You don't even know what a tree lighting is."

"Maybe not, but it's all I've heard people talking about for the past few minutes as I was searching for you. Did you know they're going to make it snow?"

Shreya did know. Ella had shown her how she'd created a holographic program to recreate snow on the promenade. She eyed Vox. "Don't tell me you're excited for snow."

"I do not know what it is," he said. "Should I be excited?"

"It's cold and wet."

"Hmm." He tilted his head at her. "I like wet."

Heat curled in her belly, electric sensations skating across her skin as he rubbed one thumb across her bare flesh. "Then you're in luck."

His eyes flared, then went to the drink in her hand. "Is this the first time you've had Palaxian Pleasure Tonic?"

"Palaxian what?"

"Palaxian Pleasure Tonic. It loosens inhibitions." He traced a hand down her arm. "Not that I have any when it comes to you."

She eyed her glass. That would explain why his fingertip felt electrified as it feathered across her skin. "So what will it do to me?"

She leaned closer, arching a brow at him. "Will it make me want you to fuck me even more than I already do?"

He drew in a sharp breath. "It will make you say things like *that.*"

She put a hand over her mouth and giggled. "I see what you mean. All I can think about is how much I want to ride your cock, and I don't even feel naughty saying it out loud."

Vox jerked as if jolted by electricity. "Would you like to know all I can think about?"

She rubbed up against him, practically purring. "I hope it's the same thing."

"I think back to you being tied up on Lymora III, and I wish I'd taken you then." The words rushed out of him as he stroked his finger up the underside of her bare arm. "You were so helpless, but you were so wet for me."

She met his gaze, his eyes flashing with desire. She remembered how her body had betrayed her when she'd been strapped to the X-cross and how aroused she'd been as he'd dressed her. "I wanted you to fuck me, but I didn't want to admit it. It felt so wrong to want you like that."

Vox pressed a palm to her back. "Nothing is wrong between us. You are mine now."

She nodded, releasing a breathy sigh and feeling his rigid length against her. "I was always yours."

He took the tall, glass cylinder from her hand and set it on the bar. "I don't think either of us need more of this."

Shreya let herself be led through the crowd and onto an empty inclinator compartment. When the doors slid shut and the noise of the party was drowned out, she leaned into Vox. "We won't be able to see the tree lighting from our suite."

"We aren't going to our suite."

She noticed that the inclinator was dropping instead of surging up. "Where are we—?"

He stopped her question by crushing his mouth to hers, parting her lips with a hard sweep of his tongue, and delving deep. Her head swam as he pulled her closer, pinning her arms to the small of her back and grinding his rigid length against her.

She was in a daze when the inclinator doors swished open, and he tugged her out and along a wide, sleek corridor. When they reached a set of double doors, Vox waved a hand to open them.

Shreya blinked a few times as he led her into the high-ceilinged space covered in mats, with white punching bags suspended in mid-air. She'd never seen this part of the station, but she suspected it was a gym for Drexians. The equipment was too oversized for humans or most of the other species on the station. She inhaled the scent of humidity, and suspected the officers' pool she'd heard about was nearby. "We're going to work out?"

He didn't answer as he propelled her around padded benches and racks of weights. When they stood in front of a wide, metal, ladder-looking contraption bolted to the wall, Vox pulled a long rope of glittery, gold garland from his pocket.

She knew the cocktails might have gone to her head, but she was confused. "We're going to decorate this thing?"

"Every time I see this rack, I imagine how pretty you'd look strapped to it." Grasping one of her wrists, he pulled her so she stood with her back up against the ladder, then he lifted her arm and tied it to one of the crossbeams so quickly she barely had time to register what he was doing.

"What in the bloody hell...?"

Before she could jerk her other arm away, he was kissing her hard as he strapped it over her head, as well. When he tore his mouth from hers, he was panting. "Just like I remember you on Lymora III."

Then, as like now, her body betrayed her as heat pulsed between her legs. "What if someone walks in?"

"They won't. Everyone is at the party." He unfastened the buttons running down the front of her top.

She tugged against the restraints. "I could always knee you in the balls again."

He grinned at her, opening her top and growling low when he saw the tight, dusky points of her nipples. "You won't."

"Cocky bastard," she muttered, the corners of her mouth quirking up.

He captured one nipple in his mouth and she bowed her back into him, her eyes rolling skyward. It was hard to stay angry with him when every fiber of her being was begging to be touched. Not only was she crazy about Vox, but the pleasure tonic made it impossible for her to care about anything but the fiery sensations storming through her body. She didn't even care that anyone could walk in and see her strapped to the wall, her bare breasts exposed as her big Drexian mate sucked on them. The thought of it actually made her moan out loud.

Shreya was so preoccupied—the feel of his hot, insistent mouth so intoxicating—she barely noticed Vox working the tie of her skirt with his hands until it had fallen to the floor in a pool of fabric.

He stepped back, holding her at arm's length, cupping her breasts in his hands and squeezing her nipples. "You are mine." He leaned in so his lips buzzed her ears. "Mine to take in any way I want."

She wanted to protest, but his words made her shudder with pleasure.

Bending down, he tugged her panties down the length of her legs, tossing them to the side, along with her skirt. As he straightened, he dragged his hand up her thigh and between her legs, his fingers parting her folds. "This is mine, yes?"

"Yes," she managed to whisper.

"Open your legs for me, mate," he ordered, his voice raw and dominant.

She let her legs fall open, her hips shifting impatiently as he teased the flesh of her thighs. When he found her clit, she let out a cry, dropping her head back as he circled it. She was already on the edge, and his steady strokes soon had her bucking against him.

With his other hand, he jerked his pants down and freed his cock. "Before when I had you tied up, I didn't fuck you." He dragged the crown of his cock through her folds as she quivered. "Now I will." His gaze flicked to her hands tied over her head and she strained instinctively against the sparkly makeshift restraints. He lifted her legs to hook them around his waist. "You can struggle all you want, but you can't stop me from taking what's mine."

With a single hard thrust, he buried himself inside her, his mouth crashing on hers in a primal fury. Their tongues battled as he powered into her, and his hands dug into her ass. She didn't want to love this as much as she did—being bound, being dominated—but she did. The thought of being helpless, her body pressed up hard against the metal rods with him moving hard and fast between her legs, sent heat pulsating through her body.

Clamping her legs around him, Shreya tightened her grip as she met each thrust of his huge cock. She wrapped her fingers around the bar she was tied to, unable to do anything but surrender as he claimed her, his mouth plundering hers and his cock lodging deep.

He pulled back, his face glistening with sweat. "You are mine. You have been since I carried you to the pleasure house on Lymora III." His eyes skated hungrily down her body. "Mine to claim in any way I desire."

She met his gaze defiantly, even as she tightened her legs around his waist, holding him inside her. "Cocky bastard."

He smiled, even as the veins in his neck strained and he stroked into her. "You want me to stop?"

She whimpered, as she shook her head no. She didn't want him to ever stop.

"Tell me what you want," he whispered.

She locked eyes with him, her breath escaping in desperate pants. "I want it hard."

When he knifed up and roared, her body splintered apart, writhing and convulsing as he pulsed into her.

She finally let her legs sag. They both gasped for breath, and his eyes were still wild when he looked at her. Taking the side of her face in his hand, he kissed her, this time slowly and gently.

"So beautiful," he said, touching his forehead to hers. "I still can't believe you're mine."

"Always and forever," she said, sucking in a ragged breath. "So you called it Palaxian pleasure tonic?"

He pulled back, nodding and raising an eyebrow as a bead of sweat trickled down his furrowed brow.

She squeezed him with her legs. "I think I know what I want for Christmas."

CHAPTER
FIFTEEN

"It's time, Reina." Serge rushed up to her, the tiny Perogling close on his heels, her pink wig bobbing.

Reina darted a glance over the heads as she nibbled the corner of her bottom lip. "Time for what?"

Serge put a hand on his hip as he glared up at her. "For the big event, the grand finale, the coup de grace." He paused to catch his breath. "The tree lighting, don't you remember?"

"Of course." She pressed a hand to her heart. "The tree lighting. I remember."

She also remembered that it was her job to give Ella the sign, since she was the only one tall enough to be seen over all the people. She wished her height would help her locate Vivan, but she'd been searching for him all evening, and hadn't spotted him once. He'd promised he would be at the party.

She hoped he hadn't forgotten. Touching a long finger to her hair and the tight curls that Mandy had insisted on for the occasion, she let out a sigh. The party was almost over.

"Reina!"

"Oh, yes, of course," she said, ignoring Serge's murderous stare as she spotted Ella by the base of the huge tree. She caught the woman's eye and gave her a thumbs-up. Ella nodded and tapped away at her tablet. "All done."

Serge mumbled something Reina was glad she couldn't hear over the sudden swell in music. The lights on the promenade dimmed, and the tree went dark before twinkling lights lit up at the bottom and swirled around until they reached the top. The star then blinked and holographic sparks shot from it, sending fireworks high in the sky where they exploded into gold and white starbursts. Instead of light falling from the fireworks, though, flakes of snow cascaded down, accompanied by oohs and ahs from the crowd below. Although it vanished before touching down, the falling snow looked magical as it filled the air.

"Perfect." Serge clapped his hands. "I knew they could do it."

Reina decided not to remind her coworker that he'd expressed doubt on numerous occasions that Ella could pull off the holographic feat on the promenade. Luckily, he and Cerise bustled off, leaving her looking up at the snow as it continued to fall.

"I am glad you did not ask me to source this snow."

Reina let out a small yelp and looked over quickly to see Vivan standing next to her. "You're here!"

He inclined his head at her. "I would say greetings of the day, but it seems it is already evening."

"Yes, the party is in full swing, as the humans—and Serge—would say." She caught herself, hoping she did not sound petulant. "Have you just arrived?"

His large, gold eyes crinkled as he smiled. "Sadly, yes. Our department has been very busy with the arrival of the Earth transport."

Reina knew about the transport. Of course, the procurement department would be busy, since many of the items they had requested from Earth would need to be inventoried before distribution. "At least you made it for the tree ceremony."

Vivan tipped his head back to gaze at the snow as it fluttered above them. "Some Earth traditions are very enjoyable."

"It's a curious little planet, but I also enjoy some of their customs." Reina forced herself to look away from him and up at the snow. "I hope we celebrate Christmas again next rotation."

Vivan rocked back on his heels. "That would be nice."

Reina's heart pounded as they stood shoulder to shoulder. They were so close, she could feel his warmth.

"I almost forgot," he said, turning abruptly. "I got you something."

She looked down at the small, red box he held in his slender hands. "Is it for one of my tribute brides?"

"No, it's for you." He cleared his throat. "It's what the humans call a Christmas present."

Her face warmed as she took the box. She didn't dare look at him for fear her cheeks were as red as they felt.

"I did some research," he said, his words fast. "This is a human tradition that only takes place around Christmas."

Lifting the shiny box top, she peered inside. "Leaves. How lovely."

Vivan chuckled. "It is called mistletoe."

"Mistle-toe," Reina repeated, plucking the small cluster of green from inside the box and inspecting the tiny white berries that clung to the stems. She remembered the humans saying something about mistletoe.

Vivan gingerly touched one of the leaves. "Anyone standing underneath it cannot refuse a kiss."

Reina fought the urge to flutter her fingers at her throat. "Oh?" She looked at him and saw that his gray cheeks were mottled pink. "Underneath it or near it?"

If it was possible for his cheeks to burn redder, they did. "I am not sure. Perhaps both?"

The mistletoe trembled in her hand, as Reina looked around her at the couples laughing, standing close, and swaying together to the music. What was it Mandy had said about taking a chance at Christmas?

Vivan looked up from staring at the mistletoe and met her gaze. "Reina?"

The way he said her name, soft and urgent, made her legs quiver. "Yes, Vivan?"

Even though the music and laughter swirled around them, she could hear nothing but his low voice and shallow breath. She closed her eyes and leaned in quickly, before she could think better of it, letting the warmth of his lips send a frisson of pleasure down her long limbs. When she opened her eyes again, Vivan was smiling at her, his entire face pink, and his lips as red as a cheedi berry.

"This is the best Christmas present I've ever gotten," she said, returning his smile and glancing at the mistletoe.

Vivan cleared his throat. "I am glad you like it."

His fingertip briefly touched hers, and Reina had to remind herself to breathe. Another cheer went up in the crowd as a second set of fireworks shot up from the top of the tree. They both watched in silence.

"This is quite a party," Vivan finally said. "The humans certainly know how to celebrate."

Reina turned to him. "Have you heard about New Year's Eve?"

He blinked and tilted his head at her. "I have not."

She steadied her breath as she recalled what Mandy had told her about midnight on New Year's Eve, her pulse quickening as she gazed into his eyes. "I think you would also enjoy New Year's traditions."

EPILOGUE

Captain Varden couldn't help smiling as he tipped his head back to see the white flakes falling seemingly out of thin air and drifting down onto the promenade, disappearing before they reached the ground. Snow, the humans called it. The holographic version of it was pretty, although he'd heard the real version was both wet and cold. This was one case where he felt the recreated version had improved significantly on reality.

The party had thinned out. Most of the Drexians had either returned to their posts or had retired for the evening, and the mated couples had disappeared long before. Now the only stragglers were those who were cleaning up, or having one last drink.

His gaze fell on someone who didn't fit either of those categories. The pretty blonde independent stood with her friend Ella near the table that held the sugary treats some of the humans called cookies and others called biscuits. She nibbled on one, catching the crumbs in one hand as she laughed. Even though her red dress covered most of her, it hugged her curves and made him stifle a groan.

True. He repeated her name in his head as he watched her finish the last bite then brush off her hands. It was the name that had filled his head since he'd met her in her beach simulation. He'd thought of little else but her since she'd mistaken him for a holographic creation and kissed him. The best kiss of his life, he reminded himself. He shifted uncomfortably as his cock twitched at the memory.

He wanted to talk to her, to be the reason she smiled and laughed. He wished he could take one of the plants the humans called mistletoe and use it to steal a kiss, like he'd seen so many mated couples do that evening. The Earth celebration of Christmas seemed to have an awful lot to do with love, if the party the tribute brides had planned was any indicator. His chest ached as he stared at True and imagined being able to take her into his arms as the snow fell on them.

Don't be a fool, he told himself. She's half your age. Plus, she was one of the females who'd specifically chosen not to take a Drexian mate. If she'd wanted, she could have had her pick of young, handsome warriors, but she'd declined. No way would she be interested in him, even if he did keep himself in excellent shape. The only reason she'd kissed him was because she'd been convinced he was part of the holographic program. The one she'd titled "Gulf of Mexico."

He thought often about returning to it, so he could feel the sand beneath his feet and the sun on his face. And, if he was being honest, so he could see her again. Her image had filled his dreams so often over the past couple of weeks that he'd almost rushed to bed each night, eager to see her. Quite a change from his usual fitful sleep, typically interrupted by worries over a Kronock invasion.

His communication device vibrated and he retrieved it from his pocket, cursing as he saw that he was being summoned back to the bridge. Sleep would have to wait. He gave one final, long look at True, the corners of his mouth twitching up at her habit of twirling a strand of hair around one finger as she talked. The faster she talked, the faster she twirled, and he found it charming.

As he spun on his heel, Varden saw her glance up. His heart thumped as he strode away, even though he was almost sure she hadn't gotten a good enough look to recognize him. He didn't slow or glance back as he entered an inclinator compartment and slid in behind a heavyset Allurian, and an alien with pale-pink skin and long, silver hair. When the doors slid shut and the compartment rose into the air, he released his breath.

Of course, it was ridiculous that he was avoiding someone on his own ship. But what would he say? *I'm sorry I pretended to be a hologram?* He doubted she would understand. He didn't know if he understood. All he knew was that he wanted the fantasy to continue a little while longer.

When the inclinator finally opened on the top floor, he took long steps toward the bridge, barely breaking stride as the wide, double doors slid open for him. It took his eyes a moment to adjust to the dark interior of the command deck, which was all black consoles and sleek metal. It was one of the few places on board the space station that wasn't bright and airy, and also one of the only places Captain Varden felt at home.

"Report," he said, seeking out his first officer at a nearby standing console.

"It's the Kronock, sir."

No shock there. "More attacks on Inferno Force?"

"Negative." His first officer turned sharply toward him. "We've received further intelligence that they are massing forces."

Grek.

This must be the invasion of Earth the Kronock had been planning. The battleships weren't jumping in so they could save their power reserves, of that he was almost certain. He could only hope the rest of Inferno Force would arrive before the aliens reached the technologically outmatched planet.

"How long until they attack Earth?" Varden asked, his hands clasped tightly behind him as he focused on the view screen overhead.

"Their target is not Earth, sir," his first officer said, his voice grim. "From what our sources say, their target is the Boat."

<small>THANK YOU FOR READING</small> JINGLED!

If you liked this alien abduction romance, you'll love CRAVED. True has no idea the gorgeous silver fox who keeps appearing in her holographic simulation is actually the station's captain. But the truth always comes out. Sometimes at the worst possible time.

One-click CRAVED Now>

"5 stars is not enough! Everyone should want a Varden."- Amazon Reviewer

This book has been edited and proofed, but typos are like little gremlins that like to sneak in when we're not looking. If you spot a typo, please report it to: tana@tanastone.com
Thank you!!

PREVIEW OF BOUNTY— BARBARIANS OF THE SAND PLANET #1

Below is a sample of another Tana Stone sci-fi-romance series—this one with alien barbarians and female bounty hunters!

Chapter One

"Are they shooting at us?" Danica asked, grabbing the edge of a smooth, metal console as she stepped onto the bridge and the ship heaved to one side. She tasted blood as she bit the inside of her mouth, and flinched from the pain. *Son of a bitch.*

She and Bexli had just brought their latest captive onboard, and she'd given the order to take off, hoping the rival bounty hunters who'd also been in pursuit hadn't seen them. From the staccato sounds of gunfire, she guessed that her plan of slipping out unnoticed was shot to hell.

She took in the familiar sight of the compact bridge—a round, flat panel console in the center of the room with view screens suspended above it, smaller individual consoles forming a half moon around the main one, and a final ring of screened consoles against the circular walls. A long, narrow slit of a window gave them a view out the front of the ship, but had a steel shade they could lower for security. Nearly every part of the room was composed of metal that was long past gleaming, and looked nearly black with age and grime. Wires spilled from underneath most of the consoles, a result of various hacks and patches to keep the aging space ship running. Danica inhaled the scent of burning fuel that seemed to permeate the ship, and felt a rush of affection for the bucket of bolts she'd practically grown up on.

"Looks like it," her pilot, Caro, said turning from one of the smaller consoles where she navigated the ship, her straight, nearly black hair flying behind her as she spun back around. "And we're definitely outgunned."

"Can we outrun them?" Danica asked, as she made her way down to the center console and looked out at the massive ship blocking their escape.

"What we don't have in size or gun power, we make up for in maneuverability," Caro said. "I should be able to get a little extra acceleration from our impulse drives if I boost the—"

"Caro," Danica said, cutting off the woman before she launched into an overly detailed explanation of their engine.

"Sorry, Captain," Caro said spinning back around to her console. "On it."

"I hope you're right," Tori said from where she stood at the weapons console along the wall, her curly, dark hair pulled up in a topknot and held in place with what looked like metal chopsticks with dangerously sharp ends—almost as sharp as her pointy teeth. A row of hard, raised bumps ran above her eyebrows, down along the sides of her face and disappeared into her hairline—a hallmark of the Zevrians—making her look even fiercer than she was. "Because we're running low on weapons."

"How low?" Danica gripped the console with both hands as the ship jerked to the right and skirted underneath the larger ship.

"How good are you at hand-to-hand combat?" Tori asked, her brown, muscled arms braced against the wall.

Danica had gotten a lot of flak—mostly from her father's old bounty-hunter friends—when she'd brought on the Zevrian as her security chief, but she'd never had a moment's regret for making Tori a part of her team. Especially in situations like these.

"I thought we were supposed to stock up when we were docked at Centuri Twelve," Danica shouted over the roar of the engines firing.

"I would have, if we had anything to buy them with," Tori said as the ship accelerated.

Danica sighed. Her crew had been running on fumes—sometimes literally—for weeks. "I know it's been tight, but once we turn over this bounty, we'll be flush for a while."

"I'm just glad Mourad won't have the satisfaction of beating us." Caro turned to face forward as the force of acceleration pressed her back into her chair. "I hate that guy."

Danica couldn't agree more. The ship shooting at them belonged to a bounty hunter and mercenary named Mourad, who didn't believe in female bounty hunters and didn't believe in playing fair. Not that Danica was against stretching the rules or pushing her luck, but Mourad had no limits on what he and his crew would do to capture a bounty.

He was the one bounty hunter her father had gone out of his way to avoid, because Mourad ignored all the usual professional courtesies and accepted practices. He would double-cross anyone. Instead of tracking down bounties himself, he was known for waiting until another bounty hunter did all the legwork, then he and his band of mercenaries would swoop in and snake the bounty. Just like he was trying to do now.

Over my dead body, Danica thought, as their ship broke through the atmosphere and shot into space, the sky going from hazy yellow to inky blue to black. She thumped the side of the console, mentally thanking the ship for getting her out of yet another scrape.

When her father died, he'd left everything to her, which meant basically his ship. It had just been the three of them for as long as Danica could remember—her and her father and the ship. Different crews had come and gone, but the ship had been the only constant in their lives, aside from each other. She'd thought about selling it, but only for a moment. The old ship was as much a part of her as her father had been, and she couldn't stand the thought of losing both of them.

She knew her father had never wanted her to take over his bounty-hunting business. Truth be told, he never thought it was possible, but after spending a childhood chasing after crooks all over the galaxy, she didn't really know any other life. She was good at tracking people and getting out of scrapes and skirting the law. Her father had taught her well.

Danica shook thoughts of her father out of her head as she glanced at the fuel gauge. "Good work. We should have enough steam to reach the Gendarvian outpost, where we can unload our bounty and get our reward."

Tori crossed the bridge to stand next to her, the chain belt wrapped several times around her waist jingling as she walked. "I wonder what this one did to command such a high price."

Danica shrugged, tucking a loose strand of wavy, blonde hair behind her ear. "It's not our business to wonder why. I can tell you it wasn't for a violent offense. I've never had a bounty put up less of a fight."

"The tracking was the hard part. Dr. Max Dryden did a fucking brilliant job of hiding."

The women turned to see their engineer, Holly, step onto the bridge. While the rest of Danica's crew favored utilitarian clothes that made them look more like their male counterparts—military issue pants, T-shirts, multi-pocketed vests and jackets—the ship's engineer and resident computer whiz wore color and patterns and combined them fearlessly. Red hair spilled over her shoulders and down the skintight, pink-paisley top she'd paired over an equally snug pair of turquoise pants. Her decidedly feminine appearance didn't do a thing to stop her from cursing like a space pirate, which usually startled people who thought her girly looks meant she was all sugar and spice.

"Not good enough to outfox us," Tori said, hand on her hip.

"Luckily for you, I understand the doctor's research and narrowed it down to the few planets that are ideal for that type of scientific study," Holly said. "And then Bexli did her thing."

Bexli was the other non-human in the crew. A Lycithian shape-shifter who excelled at sneaking in and out of otherwise impenetrable places, she was their ace in the hole. Officially, she was their acquisitions officer, but only in the sense that she could acquire any bounty by way of her shape-shifting skills. She was so indispensable, Danica even put up with the pet glurkin that Bexli had insisted on bringing on board.

"Remind me again what type of research," Tori said, then shook her head. "Never mind, I actually don't care."

Holly rolled her eyes at Tori. "The study of a rare mineral only found in a few systems. Word on the astronet is that the doctor has figured out a way to harness its power, which would be fucking amazing."

Caro twisted in her chair to face them. "I'm still not thrilled we're turning over a scientist. Are we sure this is a legit bounty? How many doctors do you know who commit crimes severe enough to command this amount? Should we really be turning in other women? I mean, we're an all female bounty-hunting crew."

Danica frowned, partly at Caro's barrage of questions and partly because she'd had the same thoughts, and had been trying to ignore her inner voice during the entire search. "We don't have the luxury of picking and choosing our bounties. Anyway, if we don't turn the doctor in, someone else will. At least we treat our prisoners well."

"Not that all of them deserve it." Tori pulled up the hem of her black cargo pants to reveal a thin, red scar running up her calf. "We should have put that Daxian smuggler out the airlock."

"Agreed," Bexli said, as she joined the other women on the

bridge, a tiny puff of green fur running along beside her. "He was particularly repulsive."

"Is the bounty all settled?" Danica asked.

Bexli nodded, and her iridescent-lavender bob swung at her jawbone. "This one was a breeze. I didn't even have to transform into something terrifying to keep her in line."

She leaned against a console and scooped Pog up in one arm, ruffling its fur and making it emit a low purr. "The Daxian from our last mission only stopped struggling when I morphed into a gorvon."

"Remind me again, what's a gorvon?" Holly asked.

"A particularly gruesome creature from the Daxian's home world." Bexli grinned. "Lots of claws and fangs."

Caro laughed, tightening her high ponytail. "That explains why he soiled his cell."

"At least he kept us in fuel and rations for a month," Danica said, glancing at Tori. "And you gave him a few scars, if I remember correctly."

Tori grinned. "A souvenir from the bounty hunter babes."

"You know I hate that nickname." Danica folded her arms across her chest.

"Babes is better than the other name they call us that also starts with a *b*." Holly leaned against one of the consoles, crossing her long legs at the ankles.

"I don't mind the name so much," Caro said. "At least they're talking about us."

Danica let out a long breath. "They should be talking about us because we've brought in the two highest bounties in the past astro-year, not because we're all women."

Holly patted her on the shoulder. "It's just because we're the first—and so far only—all-female bounty-hunter crew. Once the novelty wears off, or another crew comes along, people will talk about something else."

Danica knew there was truth in Holly's words, but she hated the fact that even though they'd brought in two of the toughest bounties around, the other hunters still didn't respect them. She'd known working in a field known for tough guys wouldn't be easy, but she'd hoped her unorthodox methods and maverick crew would win her respect. So far, they'd only managed to acquire nicknames.

"I say we own it," Tori said, taking one of the pointy chopsticks from her hair and pressing the needle-like point into the pad of her finger. "We know we can do any job the boys can do and, once we bring in this hot-shot doctor, we'll be rolling in enough dough to outfit this ship so we can blast anyone out of the sky. Let them call us babes then."

"Um, guys." Caro's fingers flew across the screen in front of her. "We probably shouldn't count our money quite yet."

Danica jerked her head to the screens above her, slamming her palm against the console when she saw the rival ship closing in on them. "I thought we had enough of a head start to lose them."

"They're faster than I expected for a ship that large," Caro said, maneuvering their ship so that it dipped to the left.

Holly slid onto the floor, landing with a thud. "A little warning next time."

"Sorry," Caro shouted over the sound of weapons fire hitting their hull. "You should probably brace for impact."

A blast shook the ship and alarms began screaming, red lights flashing overhead.

"Was that a torpedo?" Danica asked, shaking her head in disbelief. Was a rival bounty hunter really trying to blow up her ship?

"Shit." Holly scrambled to her feet, using the nearest console to pull herself toward the door. "I'd better get back to the engine room. If we lose that, we're dead in the water."

"I'll go make sure the prisoner is okay," Bexli said, following Holly with Pog tucked under one arm.

The entire ship jolted, and Danica heard the sound of metal scraping against metal. Her skin went cold. "They've clamped on."

Tori's face was grim. "They're boarding us."

"Maybe they'll take the doctor and go," Caro said, although her voice quivered. Danica knew her pilot had been captured more than once when she was a pilot for a resistance movement, and she suspected it hadn't always been pleasant.

Danica squeezed her hands into fists. "They're not taking our bounty or us." She turned to Tori. "Hold them off as long as you can, but don't get yourself killed. I have a plan."

Tori pulled the other chopstick from her hair and slipped both sharp metal sticks into her chain belt. "You got it, Captain."

Danica ran off the bridge and down the dimly lit corridor until she reached a steel door where Bexli stood guard. "I've got the doctor. Why don't you and Pog try to hold off Mourad's soldiers?"

Bexli nodded, her lithe frame and lavender hair transforming into a hulking beast covered in matted fur, with only the slightest hint of purple at the tips. Pog gave a gruff bark and became a green lizard the size of a human, with short legs that scampered across the floor. Both creatures hurried off toward the noise of the enemy bounty hunters boarding their ship.

Danica turned back to the steel door and punched in a code. The door slid open with a groan, revealing a petite figure with short, chocolate-brown hair sitting on the edge of a cot in the sparse room.

"Doctor Dryden," Danica said, her breath ragged. "Some pretty nasty bounty hunters are coming on board to take you. I can promise you they won't be as humane as we've been, but I have a plan that could save us both."

The woman on the cot blinked her wide, blue eyes a few times before answering. "Call me Max."

To be continued . . .

Want to read BOUNTY, book 1 in the Barbarians of the Sand Planet series? Click HERE to keep reading!

ALSO BY TANA STONE

The Tribute Brides of the Drexian Warriors Series:

TAMED (also available in AUDIO)

SEIZED (also available in AUDIO)

EXPOSED (also available in AUDIO)

RANSOMED (also available in AUDIO)

FORBIDDEN (also available in AUDIO)

BOUND (also available in AUDIO)

JINGLED (A Holiday Novella) (also in AUDIO)

CRAVED (also available in AUDIO)

STOLEN (also available in AUDIO)

SCARRED (also available in AUDIO)

ALIEN & MONSTER ONE-SHOTS:

ROGUE (also available in AUDIO)

VIXIN: STRANDED WITH AN ALIEN

SLIPPERY WHEN YETI

CHRISTMAS WITH AN ALIEN

YOOL

Raider Warlords of the Vandar Series:

POSSESSED (also available in AUDIO)

PLUNDERED (also available in AUDIO)

PILLAGED (also available in AUDIO)

PURSUED (also available in AUDIO)

PUNISHED (also available on AUDIO)

PROVOKED (also available in AUDIO)

PRODIGAL (also available in AUDIO)

PRISONER

PROTECTOR

PRINCE

The Barbarians of the Sand Planet Series:

BOUNTY (also available in AUDIO)

CAPTIVE (also available in AUDIO)

TORMENT (also available on AUDIO)

TRIBUTE (also available as AUDIO)

SAVAGE (also available in AUDIO)

CLAIM (also available on AUDIO)

CHERISH: A Holiday Baby Short (also available on AUDIO)

PRIZE (also available on AUDIO)

SECRET

RESCUE (appearing first in PETS IN SPACE #8)

Inferno Force of the Drexian Warriors:

IGNITE (also available on AUDIO)

SCORCH (also available on AUDIO)

BURN (also available on AUDIO)

BLAZE (also available on AUDIO)

FLAME (also available on AUDIO)

COMBUST

THE SKY CLAN OF THE TAORI:

SUBMIT (also available in AUDIO)

STALK (also available on AUDIO)

SEDUCE (also available on AUDIO)

SUBDUE

STORM

All the TANA STONE books available as audiobooks!

INFERNO FORCE OF THE DREXIAN WARRIORS:

IGNITE on AUDIBLE

SCORCH on AUDIBLE

BURN on AUDIBLE

BLAZE on AUDIBLE

FLAME on AUDIBLE

RAIDER WARLORDS OF THE VANDAR:

POSSESSED on AUDIBLE

PLUNDERED on AUDIBLE

PILLAGED on AUDIBLE

PURSUED on AUDIBLE

PUNISHED on AUDIBLE

PROVOKED on AUDIBLE

BARBARIANS OF THE SAND PLANET

BOUNTY on AUDIBLE

CAPTIVE on AUDIBLE

TORMENT on AUDIBLE

TRIBUTE on AUDIBLE

SAVAGE on AUDIBLE

CLAIM on AUDIBLE

CHERISH on AUDIBLE

TRIBUTE BRIDES OF THE DREXIAN WARRIORS

TAMED on AUDIBLE

SEIZED on AUDIBLE

EXPOSED on AUDIBLE

RANSOMED on AUDIBLE

FORBIDDEN on AUDIBLE

BOUND on AUDIBLE

JINGLED on AUDIBLE

CRAVED on AUDIBLE

STOLEN on AUDIBLE

SCARRED on AUDIBLE

SKY CLAN OF THE TAORI

SUBMIT on AUDIBLE

STALK on AUDIBLE

SEDUCE on AUDIBLE

ACKNOWLEDGMENTS

I hope you enjoyed this holly, jolly novella with the couples from the previous Tribute Brides of the Drexian Warriors novels. It was fun to revisit them and let them have a little holiday fun! The series will continue with True and Varden's story, as well as the adventures of the newly-arrived tribute brides. Stay tuned!

My deepest thanks to all my readers and to everyone who's given me a lovely review, emailed me, or reached out on social media. You are the BEST!

Wishing everyone a Merry Christmas, Happy Hanukkah, or Happy Kwanzaa!

ABOUT THE AUTHOR

Tana Stone is a USA Today bestselling sci-fi romance author who loves sexy aliens and independent heroines. Her favorite superhero is Thor (with Aquaman a close second because, well, Jason Momoa), her favorite dessert is key lime pie (okay, fine, *all* pie), and she loves Star Wars and Star Trek equally. She still laments the loss of *Firefly*.

She has one husband, two teenagers, and two neurotic cats. She sometimes wishes she could teleport to a holographic space station like the one in her tribute brides series (or maybe vacation at the oasis with the sand planet barbarians). :-)

She loves hearing from readers! Email her any questions or comments at tana@tanastone.com.

Want to join her VIP Readers list and be the first to know about contests and giveaways? Click here: BookHip.com/CRJHNH

Want to hang out with Tana in her private Facebook group? Join on all the fun at: https://www.facebook.com/groups/tanastonestributes/

facebook.com/tanastoneauthor
instagram.com/tanastoneauthor
bookbub.com/authors/tana-stone
amazon.com/Tana-Stone/e/B07V3LRSNH

Printed in Great Britain
by Amazon

41841222R00067